To Joan
with best wishes

Bernd Dietz

THE ANTELOPE PLAY

A Novel
BOYD TAYLOR

Katherine Brown Press
Austin, TX
KBTPress@ymail.com

First Printing 2013

ISBN 9780989470704

Library of Congress Control Number
2013942073

Printed in the United States of America
by Lightning Source

TO KITTY, ALWAYS LOVING,
ALWAYS KIND

ACKNOWLEDGEMENTS

I am especially grateful to Susan Madden for her eagle-eye and cogent comments, which helped me enormously with this book. I also thank Jack Rosshirt for reading the draft and providing thoughtful suggestions; Mindy Reed and Danielle Hartman Acee of The Authors' Assistant for their invaluable editorial and production expertise; Douglas Brown for his cover design; and of course to Katherine Brown for her encouragement and support. They all deserve credit for any merit the book may have, but, of course, the responsibility for errors or shortcomings is entirely mine.

Jan Bodgett's "Land of Bright Promise – Advertising the Texas Panhandle and South Plains, 1870-1917" (University of Texas Press, 1988) is a great resource for those interested in the marketing of the Panhandle. To my Pampa friends, I can only say that the people and places in my book are fictitious, and the history I recite is not a recounting of the actual settlement of Pampa or Gray County.

There are numerous accounts of the poisoning of Russian KGB agent Alexander Litvinenko on the Internet, and numerous newspaper and television reports are available for those interested in learning more about that event.

Oh, give me a home where the Buffalo roam

Where the Deer and the Antelope play;

Where seldom is heard a discouraging word,

And the sky is not cloudy all day.

Dr. Brewster Higley (1876)

PLAY - The activities associated with petroleum development in an area.

OilGas Glossary 2007-2013

The full moon cast shadows from the bare trees that lined the gravel road on the other side of the cattle guard. The winter wind had died down into its midnight quiet, and the cold air was settling over the arroyos, covering the low indentions in the ranch land with a light frost. A black Cadillac SUV pulled up by the cattle guard. Two men jumped out of the back of the SUV. They wore heavy coats and their hats were pulled down low on their heads. Without speaking, they pulled the motionless man out of the back seat, bumping his head on the hard dirt. "Ten cuidado!" one said. "Lo queremos vivo."

The man moaned. They took him, one by the shoulders, the other by the feet, and tossed him onto the road in front of the cattle guard. They stripped off his boots and socks and threw them in the back of the Cadillac.

"Vamos!" one of them said. They jumped in the SUV and drove away quickly; its black outline disappeared down the country road.

The sun was barely visible over the eastern plateau when the man awoke, shivering from the cold. He struggled to his feet. He hopped across the cattle guard in his bare feet and cried out in pain. When he was finally across, he rested a minute. Then, breathing heavily, he began his walk up the gravel road. He wiped blood from his nose and mouth, held his broken left arm with his right hand, and slowly walked home.

CHAPTER ONE

The address read, "Don R. Cuinn, Attorney at Law," so it had to be for him. Don looked at the legal-size envelope and sighed. He recognized the scrawled Las Vegas return address. *What now?* He tossed the unopened envelope on the pile of documents that Faye had stacked neatly before leaving the office the night before. When the envelope hit the stack, the papers scattered.

He ignored the mess and swiveled in his worn leather chair, passed on to him when Jake got new stuff, and stared through the dusty window at the brown Texas Panhandle landscape. From his aerie on the top floor, the fifth floor of Velda's tallest building, he could see the end of town to the north where it gave way to the flat land and canyons and dry creeks that stretched to Canada. He couldn't see his apartment, back to the east, toward the Country Club, and it bothered him. *Why do I care?*

He couldn't admit it bothered him because Jake, the Rosen of "Rosen & Associates" had the prime corner office, with windows to the east as well as the north, from which he could keep an eye on all of Velda that mattered: the business district, the city hall, the courthouse, the old residential district, the winding parks and dry creek, and the leafless trees. Not to mention the new developments, both of them, where wealthy Veldanians had built McMansions too big for the lots, like overweight teenagers with their exposed bellies overflowing their jeans at the Arcadia Theater or the mall in Amarillo.

But Don R. Cuinn, the associate in "Rosen & Associates," could only see to the north, and like everything else today, it grated on his nerves. *I'm in a crappy mood. What's new? Not a thing.*

Don could not see to the south, *thank God*, so he didn't have to look every day at the old warehouse district and railroad tracks, the recently repainted depot reclaimed as a half-assed museum, where the early days of Velda were trumpeted to the five visitors a week. *In a good week*, he thought. The days when Velda was an important stop on the railroad; when early settlers came to try their luck raising cotton or wheat on the unforgiving Panhandle plains; when most of the farmers were ruined by flooding rains followed by unbelievable drought, forced to sell their land, in which they had invested their life savings, sell it for pennies on the dollar to cattle ranchers. The ranchers, over a decade or two, ended up with most of the land in Velda County, and with the land, the oil money when the boom came.

South of the tracks were the Flats, with its shanty towns and trailer parks, where Velda's Hispanics and its few blacks and its oil field trash lived uneasily next to each other, huddled against the north wind all winter. And, during the rest of the year, were unable to escape the ceaseless southwest wind or the acetic acid fumes blown over them from the Crackstone Industries' chemical plant.

Lovely, Don thought.

He shivered. The cold wind leaked into his office, even with the windows painted shut. There was no way to open them in the summer and fall, when the weather was mild and dry and the wind was light enough to be enjoyable. Almost. Even sealed, the windows leaked cold air in the winter and dust in the spring. He selected an old wool sweater from the various pieces of outdoor clothing he kept on the hook behind his door. He put it on, and his corduroy jacket over it, but he was still cold. He had never been this cold growing up in Austin.

He thought of the warm days in Beaumont, where he got his diploma mill law license. *Why did I leave? Oh yes, no job.* Not even an offer. Law firms knew the worth of a J.D. degree from the Jefferson Davis School of Law. . . warm weather. . . an image of Mexico City flashed through his mind. *Not that. Don't think about that. Not for an instant.*

He heard the elevator slowly climbing to the fifth floor. He looked at his watch. *Seven thirty. That would be Faye.* He heard her open the hall door.

She called out, "Morning. Mr. Cuinn?"

"I'm here, Faye. Freezing my butt off."

He thought about straightening the stack of papers before Faye saw the mess he had made and then decided against it. For all the time he had been Jake Rosen's associate, Faye had lectured him about the virtue of a clean desk, but lately there was a resignation about her complaints. One of his few joys in coming to work every day was to listen to her complaints, and he was sorry they were becoming perfunctory. He liked Faye. She was one of the few people he did like in this town.

Even on the rare afternoons when his desk was clear, he made a point of throwing some files around so he could hear Faye say the next morning, "Oh, for goodness sakes, Mr. Cuinn. What am I going to do with you?"

The rail-thin widow set a cup of hot coffee on his desk. She looked at the files. Just as he had hoped, she said, "I'll swear, Mr. Cuinn. What am I going to do with you?"

"Run away with me, Faye. Let's leave all this behind."

She sniffed and touched her straight gray hair. She resisted the mile high hairdo, the specialty of Jean's Cuts. "Beauty parlor takes too much time," she told him once. "Plus all the gossip. The women there want to know everything I know and they get peeved when I won't tell them. Fewer hurt feelings this way."

She re-stacked his files and ran her dust cloth over the old oak desk. "That's better." She handed him a thin file. "Trey Pervoy called about this yesterday after you left. I told him it would be filed today."

He opened the file to the divorce petition Faye had drafted, using his notes. She was the best drafter of legal documents in the office. Once he had suggested a wording change, and Faye made it, but with a look that told him all he needed to know. Now he read her drafts, but he didn't quibble. He doubted if Jake even read them before scribbling his name on them as attorney of record.

The divorce petition was for Belle Mada Pervoy, a petroleum princess, the spoiled sister of the most important of Jake's rancher clients. Predictably, Belle Mada had tired of her penniless rodeo boyfriend, Tipp Newton, who never won a rodeo event, but got the grand prize when he won Belle Mada. He quit competing once he had his bride to buy him beer and pay for his rodeo circuit trips. According to the petition, the marriage had only lasted two years. He looked at the pre-nup that Jake had prepared in anticipation of this very day. By a combination of trusts, transfers of assets, and disclaimers signed by the eager-to-marry Tipp Newton, Jake had made sure the cowboy had no

4

claim on Belle Mada's interest in the Pervoy Ranch; the royalties and minerals; the house the George Pervoy Family Trust built for the couple on Country Club Gulch; the bride's jewelry; the cars; the new cutting horse she had bought her fiancée as a wedding gift; none of that or anything else, except the groom's pick-up truck and ten thousand dollars get–out-of-town money.

At least the boy had the good sense not to contest the divorce. No lawyer in Velda would think of crossing the Pervoys. Tipp threaten to hire an Amarillo lawyer to contest the pre-nup, but when he found out that the retainer coincidentally was also ten thousand dollars, he got quiet and surly and signed the papers that Don took to him at his mother's trailer house in the Flats.

Don signed the divorce petition and handed it to Faye.

She looked it over, checking it one last time. "I'll make the file copies and have Bobby take it over to the clerk's office."

"Where is he anyway?" Bobby was the law firm's errand boy, process server, auto repossessor, and driver.

Faye sighed. "Late. His excuse will be that he drove Mr. Rosen to Amarillo to catch the last flight to Dallas, but I know for a fact that the plane left at six o'clock."

"He may be at the courthouse, waiting for somebody to bail out Eugene. Has the sheriff called?"

Faye sighed again, even louder. She went into her office and checked the office's messages. "Oh, Lord," she said. "The sheriff called Mr. Rosen early yesterday morning. He tried to get you. Didn't you pick up your calls?"

5

Don shook his head. "I don't do jailhouse runs." He had seen "Velda County Sheriff's Department" on the caller ID and had turned over and gone back to sleep. *I'll be damned if I'll hike over there in the middle of the night. Not on what Jake pays me.* Then he had forgotten about the call when he woke up. *Probably not good.*

"If you want the Pervoy family business when Mr. Rosen retires, you'll have to change your mind about that."

Don snorted. He didn't have to state the obvious. *There was no way Jake Rosen would ever retire.*

Before he could speak, Faye waved him off, listening to the other messages. "You were right," she said with a grimace. "Bobby is at the jail waiting to drive Eugene home. Eugene has been in jail since early Sunday morning. You'd better get right over there. I'll call Scoot to meet you to make bail."

Scowling, Don put on his long leather coat and his black cowboy hat.

"File this divorce petition while you're over there." She handed him the file.

"Christ, Faye. When will Jake be back?"

"When he's good and ready, I imagine."

Jake was in Dallas for one of his monthly client conferences with a wealthy Dallas widow, who looked to Jake for advice and comfort. Mostly comfort, Don suspected. He didn't know and didn't want to know.

He thrust the petition into his briefcase. "Damn Pervoys. How can one family cause so much trouble?"

"Be glad they do," Faye said, turning back to her desk. *Probably going to crank out another invoice*, Don thought.

6

He decided to take the stairs rather than wait for the creaky elevator. It was the morning rush hour in Velda, and the Crackstone engineers and accountants would be straggling into work, sour faced and full of ill-tempered jokes. He opened the door and glanced to his left where Major Hansard's offices and penthouse apartment filled the other half of the fifth floor. The height-challenged Major no doubt enjoyed standing on a step-stool to look down at the town he had built—that is when he wasn't racing around it in his Mercedes 600. He and Jake jointly owned the building, and had christened it "The HanRo Building." They rented the rest of the space to Crackstone Industries, which used it as its Western Office headquarters, and to the Pervoys for their in-town ranch office.

Don bounded down the bare concrete steps, two at a time, past the Crackstone floors. He opened the stairwell door into the lobby. The lights were on in the Pervoy Ranch office. A lone accountant manned the office, except on days when Trey Pervoy graced the HanRo Building with his presence.

Don nodded at several of the arriving Crackstone employees. One overweight middle manager, who looked like a personnel department type, was carrying a cup of coffee from The Greeks. *No Starbucks in Velda. Probably the only population center of twenty thousand people where that was true.* The thing was, Don Cuinn never liked Starbucks, never went there in Austin, where there was one at each intersection. Even so, he resented like hell that he lived in a place without a Starbucks. Some weekends he would drive to Amarillo just to have a four-dollar cup of dark Sumatra and nurse his grudge against Velda.

7

He gave a mock salute to Bill Byrnes, a Crackstone middle manager. He had handled a house closing for Bill and his wife a few months back. Not a bad guy, but according to Jake, Bill had paid too much for the house.

Don pushed against the revolving glass doors and felt the full force of the north wind. He could hardly move the doors. Outside at last, he caught his hat before it blew away. He hunched over and fought against the wind for the two blocks to the courthouse. The streets were deserted. Most of downtown retail had moved to the strip mall on the west side of town, along the by-pass. *What did they think they were by-passing?*

Sheriff Boom Gordon and his wife Bessie lived in an apartment on the first floor of the courthouse annex. The annex housed the county jail, built in the 1930s to accommodate the crime wave that spilled over into the peaceful town of Velda from the oil boomtown of Borger. The apartment was situated so that any felon trying to escape from jail would have to pass through the Gordon's living room, where Boom usually sat in his overstuffed recliner watching Fox News, his shotgun at the ready beside him. If Boom had to leave the apartment, to seek out a criminal on the run, or to go to a sheriffs' convention downstate, Bessie took his place in the recliner. No convict of moderately sound mind would attempt to escape when Miz Bessie was on duty. She was renowned as a sharpshooter as well as a cook, and many said she could outshoot her husband.

The apartment was updated every ten years or so, which meant it had been painted and the appliances replaced three times since Boom was first elected sheriff. The recliner had been replaced

8

more often, because Boom and Bessie each weighed close to three hundred pounds, and even the best chair that the county commissioners could buy only lasted a year or two.

As Don expected, he found Eugene Pervoy sitting at the kitchen table, eating breakfast. Miz Bessie cooked for all the inmates, but only a few regulars got to eat in the kitchen rather than in their cells. Eugene Pervoy was one of the privileged few.

Eugene looked up. "Want some biscuits and gravy, Cuinn?" he asked.

Don took off his hat and nodded to the sheriff and his wife. "No, thanks."

Boom turned away from the apocalyptic morning news. He lay back in the recliner; his scuffed cowboy boots were propped on the foot rest; his iron belly protruded over the massive silver belt buckle and two-inch wide leather belt; his cowboy hat was pulled down to shade his eyes. "Now wait a damn minute, Eugene. Just because you're here once a week don't mean you can offer breakfast to any jake-leg lawyer that drops in."

"Hush, Sheriff," his wife said, handing Don a steaming cup of black coffee. She wore a neat apron and an old style print dress that draped over her like a tent.

"Thanks Miz Bessie. I'm frozen."

"Sit under that vent. That'll warm you up." Bessie was inordinately proud of the central gas heat that was a part of the most recent renovation.

He pulled his chair under the vent and tried to shake off the cold. He looked at Eugene. The rangy West Texan needed a shave and a shower. His hair was mussed. He could have used one of Ginelle's home haircuts. His shirt was wrinkled. He

9

had probably slept in his clothes all night. *Boom ought to provide pajamas for his regulars.*

"Well?" Cuinn asked.

Eugene mopped his plate with the last of his biscuit. "Well what?"

"Well what happened this time?"

Eugene shook his head. "I hate all these questions. Where's Lawyer Jake? He never asks all these questions."

"Jake's in Dallas. Do you want to wait until he gets back or do you want to tell me what happened?"

Eugene held out his cup to Bessie, and she filled it with fresh coffee. "Thank you, Miz Bessie." He shook his head again. "God knows how long he'll be down there with that new widow of his. I guess you're all I've got." He looked at Don with bloodshot eyes. "No Jew. Just you."

Don shook his head ruefully. "That's cold, Eugene."

"Get me out of here. I need to get out to the ranch. We've got a delivery of semen today."

Don paused, trying to get that image out of his mind. After a bit, he asked, "Who caught him this time, Boom?"

The sheriff, who was immersed in a missing dog story on Fox, didn't turn from the TV, but said, "Curtis, that city cop, noticed Eugene on Country Club Gulch weaving from side to side and driving suspiciously slow."

"Is that right, Eugene? Were you driving suspiciously slow?"

Eugene stood up and stretched. "Damn if I remember a thing. Must have been that medicine I was on."

"What medicine is that, Eugene?"

10

"You'll have to ask Lawyer Jake the name. Anyway, it has the exact same effect on a person as if he'd had six beers with whiskey chasers at the Country Club."

Don nodded. "I see." He checked his phone. "Scoot's made bail. You're a free man. Bobby is outside. He'll drive you home. Want us to pick up your truck?"

"All right with me. Thinking about getting a new one, though. This one weaves from side to side too much. Be sure and mention that to Lawyer Jake."

"Oh, I'll be sure to do that." Don was glad it would be Jake who had to negotiate with Richard Cator, the district attorney. He didn't know the drill. It may have involved contributions to Cator's re-election campaign. All Don knew was that Jake endowed many local office holders with money, money that Don suspected was reflected on the ranchers' monthly billings as tax deductible legal expenses. However he did it, Jake managed to have Eugene's weekend escapades reduced to non-moving traffic violations and a fine. The older policemen usually just drove Eugene home, but sometimes there was a new cop, like this weekend, or a state trooper, and Eugene had to spend the night watching TV with Boom and Miz Bessie.

Don was also glad he didn't have Eugene's hangover, because he had heard that Eugene's plump wife, Ginelle, had a temper and that she didn't approve of her husband sleeping somewhere else, even if he did say it was at the jail. The last time, Jake had to write a note assuring Ginelle that her husband had in fact been in police custody, and not shacked up with some fortune hunter he met at the Country Club bar: The same bar where Eugene and Ginelle met.

CHAPTER TWO

They thanked Miz Bessie and Boom and left through the side door. Bobby was waiting in the law firm's Land Cruiser. Bobby Bill McCathey was a scrawny former cowboy. When he was kicked in the head by a wayward bull at the Pervoy Ranch and almost died, Jake settled any claim the cowboy might have had against the Pervoys by putting Bobby on the law firm's payroll.

"We needed somebody" Jake justified. "He may be a little addled but he can still drive, and there's nobody better at sneaking into some old boy's yard in the Flats and bringing back his truck. Thing is, he's fearless...or doesn't know any better."

Jake had grinned his, "I got the better of you" grin and allowed, "Besides, I bill one hundred per cent of his wages to the Pervoys. Way better deal for them than paying a personal injury claim."

As if Bobby would ever have sued the Pervoys. Or would have won the lawsuit if he had sued, Don had wanted to say, but he just nodded. *That's between Jake and the Pervoys,* "Take us out to the Gulch, Bobby. We'll pick up Eugene's truck and I'll follow you out to the ranch." *Maybe the ride will get me in a better mood,* Don thought, but he doubted it.

Eugene and Ginelle lived in the original house on the Pervoy Ranch. Pete Pervoy, Eugene's great-grandfather, moved into the dugout that the original farmer had carved out of the caliche when Pete bought out the wannabe wheat farmer. It was the first tract in what today was the Pervoy Ranch. The farmer sold the land to Pete Pervoy for just enough to buy train tickets to send his wife and four

13

children back to Indiana. He saw them off at the station, then went to the farm, dug himself a grave and shot himself in the head.

Pete Pervoy lived in the dugout with his family, and later so did his eldest son, the first George Pervoy. Over the next decade, the Pervoys built and then enlarged a rock house around the original dugout; the dugout now served Eugene and Ginelle as a combination root cellar and tornado shelter. When George Pervoy II brought his new wife, Mary Marie, back to Velda, her first project was to build a new house, a replica of the house she grew up in, back in Longview. It in turn was a replica of the plantation house where her mother had lived as a young girl in Alabama. Or at least so the story went.

Eugene and Ginelle were happy with the old house. It was big enough for their growing family. It was close enough to the big house for Mary Marie to know what was going on, but far enough away that the grandkids didn't interfere with her afternoon teas, piano recitals and bridge parties. It was a pretty good bet that Mary Marie wouldn't drop in for a visit with her least favorite daughter-in-law. If she had a pronouncement to make, she would send it through the ancient black maid she had brought with her from Longview. In extreme cases, such as a complaint that Eugene's children needed a town haircut or a trip to the dentist, she would summon Eugene to the big house for instructions. Most of them Eugene simply ignored.

In addition to Eugene and his about-to-be-divorced sister, Belle Mada, there was another son, Eugene's younger brother George III, who everyone called Trey. George II died of a stroke while trying to drag a calf out of a sinkhole. Since then, the hopes of the Pervoy family rested on Trey. The brothers were not alike in any way that Don could decipher. Eugene was tall and pale like his mother, skinny, happy to live the cowboy life, in love with his wife and proud of his growing brood. His main weakness was his weekend carousing, which involved drinking until he was unconscious. *Maybe growing up with Mary Marie for a mother required that,* Don thought.

Trey was stocky and muscular, dark-haired and pugnacious like his father, ambitious and a sharp trader. He was proud of his wife Margaret, but he was not above keeping a mistress, a pretty bank trust department officer, in an upscale apartment in Amarillo.

Trey had been educated at Oklahoma University, where he played baseball and met Margaret Aspen, who was wealthy in her own right. It was a match made in Rancher Heaven, with a wedding at the Trinity Episcopal Church in Tulsa and a reception at The Oaks Country Club.

Margaret arrived in Velda as wife of the heir apparent of Velda's leading family; she stepped into her role with ease. She followed her mother-in-law's example and insisted that Trey build them their own house, but the young couple's house was a sprawling, contemporary pile on a canyon hilltop, designed by someone from the Frank Lloyd Wright studio in Arizona. Trey and Margaret's two children, George IV, called Quatro, and Mary Marie, called Junior, as befitting the offspring of the prince and princess royal, got their grandmother's special affection and attention. "Nobody ever accused Margaret of not knowing how to name kids," Jake had told Don.

15

Unlike Trey, Eugene never liked school and chose to stay home and work the ranch rather than go to college. When he and Ginelle eloped one Mother's Day, Mary Marie told Jake Rosen to get the marriage annulled. It was one of Jake's few failures, and Don suspected that Jake didn't have his heart in the annulment. He may have had a secret affection for the young couple, but he just told Mary Marie that Eugene was stubborn. The pair still loved each other and had produced three roly-poly children, who were named Kansas City (or K.C.), Dallas and San Fran for the cities where they were conceived.

Bobby opened the ranch gate, pulled the Land Cruiser onto the gravel ranch road and waited for Don to drive Eugene's pick-up through the gate. From Eugene's truck, Don could see a few cattle off to the south, but the Pervoy Ranch was mainly miles of caliche canyons and plateaus, blessed with tall grass the years that it rained, but dusty and blowing the other years.

Wellheads of gas wells and pump jacks of oil wells punctuated the view. Even though the wells provided millions of dollars to the Pervoy Family Trust, and so to the Pervoy heirs, each year, Trey regularly came to the law office demanding that Jake file a lawsuit against one of the oil companies that operated on the ranch for disturbing his *cattle ranch.*

"The only thing the damned cattle's good for is tax write-offs and so Trey can pretend he's a cattleman," Jake told Don one afternoon. Jake had just spent an hour listening to Trey complain about the damage to the ranch's roads and ponds by an

oil company that was reworking some wells on the family ranch.

"Now, George," Jake went on, referring to George II, Trey's father, "never kidded himself about that. He knew that without the oil, the damned ranch isn't worth spit."

The preceding Friday, Don heard Jake and Trey arguing in Jake's office. Their voices were louder than usual. Even Jake seemed to have lost his temper, something Don had never heard him do with any of the Pervoys, no matter how infuriated he might be. "Dammit, Trey," Don heard him say, "You are a trustee. There's limits..."

"I know I'm the trustee, and the trust will have a different lawyer, if you don't take care of this!"

Trey had slammed the door on the way out and then Don heard Jake tell Faye to book him to Dallas right away.

Don knew that Jake would not risk his Pervoy Ranch business. The ranch's dealings with the oil companies engendered mountains of legal work for Rosen and Associates. Jake Rosen was a great success as the Pervoy's lawyer, negotiating leases, trading shrewdly for record bonuses and royalties, carefully inserting landowner friendly provisions in their oil and gas leases, guiding litigation if need be, all the while using his formidable trading skills to threaten, cajole, and finally outsmart the battalions of oil company land men and Houston lawyers. Jake was never happy until he had squeezed the last penny out of every transaction, no matter how small or how large. He was unstoppable.

17

Rosen was also a tax whiz, keeping tax specialists on Pervoy Ranch retainers in Dallas and Washington. He drew up the family's wills, handled the probates, cleaned up the family's messes and kept a lid on its dirty linen.

Jake did the same kind of work for the other prominent ranching families that, along with the Pervoys, controlled most of the county.

It was a measure of his skill and energy that, for a long time, he could handle all the business alone. Finally, he felt compelled to seek an associate. "Damn it, boy," he told Don Cuinn when he interviewed him at the Dallas airport, "I'm covered up with their crap. I need me a good associate, someone to take some of the burden off this old man, take over the whole shit and shebang in a few years."

Don had not managed to get a single interview before the one with Rosen. Worse yet, he had been warned. His godfather, Professor Ralph Rothschild, came down from Austin to comfort Don when he moved to Beaumont from Mexico City. Papa did not favor Don going to law school, and especially the Beaumont diploma mill where Don had enrolled.

"Are you sure you are not being injudicious?" he asked. He carefully folded his tweed jacket, much too warm for Beaumont, and said, "Come back to Austin. Continue your work in History. You almost have your doctorate."

Don had shrugged. "I can't go back, to Austin, or to grad school. Too many memories."

Papa didn't press him on exactly what had happened to his wife in Mexico. He knew his step-son well enough not to ask for details. He smoothed his graying mustache, adjusted his shirtsleeves and sighed. "Very well Donnie. Do you need money? Is there enough left from Lena's insurance policy to see you through?" He spread his arms, smiling ruefully. Lena was Papa's deceased wife, Donnie's stepmother, who had provided him with a small legacy.

"There's more than enough, Papa, but thank you."

Papa also didn't ask why Don had not tried harder to get into a "better" law school, and Don was glad, because all he could have told him was that when he landed at Houston International, he saw an ad for the Jefferson Davis School of Law and thought, Why not? It's as good as anything else. At least it'll keep me busy for awhile.

And it had. No one cared, but Don was the outstanding student in Jeff Davis' short history of handing out degrees to underprepared minorities and city policemen taking the night school curriculum. Don did both day school and night school, drowning himself in the minutiae of the Common Law and Con Law and Contracts, anything the place offered. He graduated in two years. Anything to keep the memories of Cecilia at bay. He couldn't sleep much anyway. By the time he graduated, he had the world-weariness of a longtime practitioner and there were gray flecks in his sandy hair. He was startled when he looked at himself in the mirror. Who is this guy, with the sad, tired, blue eyes? Lena had always said he looked like a young Robert Redford. Not anymore.

He needed a job after graduation, but even his sterling record did not get him an interview. He wondered if his brief celebrity as the author of an expose of the former attorney general for This Texas poisoned the well with conservative law

19

firms, but he doubted it. His former political allies owed him a favor, so they had said, but he refused to call them. He despised them.

One person he didn't despise, though, was Drayton Philby, the blind publisher of *This Texas*, who had guided him through his confrontation with the Attorney General. So, his cash dwindling fast, he called Philby. As such things often happen, Philby knew Jake Rosen and knew that Rosen was looking for an associate to come to Velda.

"Unfortunately, it is in Velda!" Don had heard the warning in Philby's voice. "Velda, Texas! In the Texas Panhandle! You do know where the Texas Panhandle is, don't you?"

"It's never come up," Don admitted.

"It's a garden spot." When he didn't get a reply, Philby went on, more subdued this time. "It's in the middle of nowhere, but it's a job, my boy, and Jake Rosen is an excellent lawyer. You could do a lot worse, Donnie. Call Jake."

Don thought the middle of nowhere might suit him just fine. He made the call.

Faye's flat West Texas accent didn't disguise her pleasure. "Mr. Cuinn? I'm sure Mr. Rosen would like to meet with you. Are you planning to be in Dallas anytime soon?"

After some low-keyed haggling, the Rosen firm bought Donnie a round-trip coach ticket to Dallas with directions to the United First Class Lounge. The good-looking woman at the desk smiled and directed him to a small glass-enclosed conference room. "Mr. Rosen is expecting you."

Jake Rosen was talking on a cell phone. He had his legs crossed. His alligator boots glistened. He was probably in his fifties. He was swarthy and reasonably trim. He said a few soft words, closed the phone and stood up to greet Don. His black eyes twinkled. "Don Cuinn, I believe. *Boker tov. Na'im me'od .*"

Donnie grinned sheepishly as he shook Rosen's outstretched hand. "Sorry. I don't speak Hebrew, but I imagine my response is 'Good morning. Happy to meet you.'"

Rosen motioned for Donnie to sit down. "You don't? I'll tell you a secret. Neither do I. I do have a few phrases, though. I'll teach them to you if we end up working together. Sit, sit."

He eyed Donnie before he said genially, "So you're the kid who wrote that article. The article that ran Eben Payne out of Austin."

Donnie squirmed a little. "I guess Drayton told you about that."

"That can be our little secret. It wouldn't help you a lot in Velda."

"They're conservative up there?"

Jake grinned. "Forever. The John Birch Society, the nutcases back when Kennedy was shot?"

"I don't think I've heard of them."

"Way before your time. And mine. It was big back in the sixties, don't pay your income tax, it's unconstitutional, things like that. Anyway, it started in Velda. The Tea Party has five chapters in the Panhandle. And they're the moderates."

"Mum's the word." Donnie looked up at the young waitress who had been hovering nearby. "Just some water."

Jake shook his head. "No, no. Join me." He lifted up his tumbler of Scotch. "Have a drink. It isn't every day you make a decision that will affect the rest of your life, Don."

Donnie nodded. "I'll have what he's having."

21

"Double Bladnoch, neat, no ice?"

"I guess so."

Jake sipped his drink until the girl came back with the Scotch. Donnie took a small taste. He had drunk a lot of Scotch ordered by his former best friend, All-American Wesley Bird, so he knew fairly well what to expect. He took a second sip, then nodded to Jake. "Single malt, Highland?"

"Yes, of course. Know anything about Scotch, you'd know that much. Still, I guess I'm impressed." He motioned to the waitress for another.

Donnie covered his glass. "I'm good."

"Tell me one thing, Don," Jake said, cleaning a spot off his glass with his cocktail napkin, "Where the hell is Jefferson Davis Law School?"

Donnie smiled. "It's the pride and joy of the Upper Gulf Coast. Beaumont."

"Beaumont? Jesus Christ. Why there?"

"Well, they took me. I doubt that Harvard would have."

"Really? They took me. You're a smart guy. You know your Scotch. How about UT? Or Baylor? Or even Houston?"

Donnie hesitated. "I really don't know. I needed a change."

Jake shook his head. "Shit, Don, you got one." He stared at Donnie. "Tell me about your wife...that didn't work out?"

Donnie paused. "Cecilia...my wife...we were married a few months..."

"What happened?"

"I don't want to talk about it. I want to put all that behind me, Austin. Cecilia. I want to make a fresh start."

"Drayton likes you. So do I." Jake finished his drink and stood up. "There's a job for you in Velda, Don... if you want it."

CHAPTER THREE

A large black heifer was standing in the gravel road, beside the cattle guard, staring at the two vehicles. Don threw on his brakes just in time to avoid crashing Eugene's truck into the back of the law firm's Land Cruiser. Eugene jumped out, waving his hat at the placid Black Angus. "Hooee!" he shouted. "How the hell did you get out here?"

She stared at Eugene for a minute and then decided to move, allowing them to continue the drive up the canyon to the Old House. Don looked again at the horizon. The sun was higher in the sky now; it was a cloudless winter day. The wind had died down. Don rolled down the truck's window and breathed in the cold prairie air. *No wonder the Pervoys love this place,* he thought, forgetting for a minute to be unhappy.

Ginelle must have heard them coming. She was standing in front of the ranch house with her hands on her hips. Don parked Eugene's truck and joined her beside the Land Cruiser. When Eugene got out, she leaned in the window. She had a loud voice that carried. "Thank you for bring him home in one piece, Bobby. You doing all right?"

"Yes, ma'am," Don heard him reply, ducking his head. Bobby didn't enjoy small talk. Or large talk either, for that matter.

Ginelle was a large, big-breasted woman with fluffy blond hair and naturally rosy cheeks. She had probably developed her loud voice so she could be heard over the sounds of her brood. The TV was blaring in the house. "K.C., Dallas, Fran, get out here and tell your Daddy hello, now he's home from his business trip in Velda."

25

Two fat little boys, one about six, the other a couple of years younger, both with runny noses, ran and jumped into Eugene's arms. He picked one up in each arm and turned them upside down, threatening to bounce their heads on the ground. They squealed with delight. The middle child, Dallas, was a younger version of her mother, destined to be rawboned and country pretty. She waited until Eugene put down the boys and smiled at him. Eugene picked her up and kissed her on the cheek. "How's my favorite girl?" he asked.

She put her arms around his neck and kissed him back. "K.C. missed the bus, Daddy."

Eugene laughed. "That's all right, sweetheart. He can go to school tomorrow."

Ginelle looked at Don. "Thanks for getting him out, Cuinn. That's where he was, wasn't he?"

"Boom and Miz Bessie take good care of him, you know that, Ginelle."

"I know, I know." She turned and took her husband's arm. "But I'd like to go out one Saturday night. Maybe to the Country Club, you know?"

Eugene grinned and waved goodbye to Don. "No wife of mine's going to the Country Club on Saturday night. No, sir."

Don smiled and got into the Land Cruiser with Bobby. They waved goodbye to the happy family.

K.C. and his little brother ran behind the car, waving and yelling something he couldn't understand. "Mission Accomplished," he said to Bobby. "Take it home."

He looked a last time at the couple, heads together, heading into their house, their three children running around them like playful puppies. *They were the only ones of the whole Pervoy family that he might tolerate having a meal with.* He slumped back in the seat and pulled his black hat over his eyes. He needed a nap and it was a forty-five minute drive back to Velda. He was almost content.

And then his phone rang.

"What the hell do you mean letting Eugene spend the night in jail, Cuinn?"

There goes my good mood. "Good morning to you, too, Jake. No problem. We just delivered him into Ginelle's waiting arms."

"Was she pissed? I wouldn't blame her if she was pissed."

"No more than usual. Everybody's calm." He paused for effect. "Except for you."

"Cuinn, I don't pay you good money to sleep through a Saturday night call from Trey Pervoy."

Don interrupted the lecture. "Good money?"

Jake ignored his comment. "Listen to me! You do understand that the Pervoys expect us to keep Eugene out of jail?"

"Come on, Jake. You've left him there plenty of times."

"You don't get it, do you? The only reason I leave him there is if the family says to leave him there."

"Why would they do that?"

"That's their business. Maybe he needs a lesson. Maybe they don't feel like looking at his bloodshot eyes that day. How the hell should I know? All I know is, if Trey Pervoy says get my brother out of jail tonight, you sure as hell are going to do it. Do you follow me?"

This time it was Don who ignored Jake. *I do not do late night jail house runs. Not for Trey*

Pervoy or anybody else. Except maybe Faye or Bobby.

Jake must have known not to expect contrition from his associate, and he went on with his real reason for the call. "Now listen, I need you to send Bobby over to meet the morning flight."

"You're coming home early?"

"Ooh, Sylvia's got a goddam opera deal, so I told her something important has come up. I guess it has. Trey wants to see me in the morning. Then you and I are going to have a heart-to-heart talk."

Jake hung up before Don could reply. He stared at his phone. He turned and looked at Bobby, who was whistling softly to himself. "Oh, what the hell," Don said out loud. He thought a minute. *As if I cared.* He leaned back in the seat and in a second he was asleep.

CHAPTER FOUR

Don waited in his office for Jake and Trey to finish their meeting. Don had deliberately been late getting in. He didn't want Jake to see him sitting around, waiting for the confrontation that both knew was coming.

The Pervoy heir had hobbled into the office on crutches, his arm in a sling. "What happened?" Don asked.

Trey looked at him with cold blue eyes. "Thrown," he said finally.

"By your horse?" Don managed to ask. He knew it was a stupid question before it was out of his mouth.

Trey shook his head pityingly and hopped into Jake's office. They were alone for almost an hour, talking softly. Don put on a play list from his iPod, determined not to eavesdrop. Even so, when Trey left, he heard Jake tell him, "Bring back the papers when you have everybody's signature. Signed in front of a notary. Faye can do that here if you want her to, or she can come out to the ranch and do it. Just be sure and get everybody."

"Tell me again."

"Just like I told you. You and your Mama, your sister, and Eugene. Plus you as guardian for your kids, Eugene for his, and I'll get the judge to appoint a guardian for any unborn Pervoys. We have to have everybody."

"I'll get them. Give me the goddamned papers."

Jake headed his yellow Cadillac out of downtown, on the way to the Country Club, with

Don in the passenger seat. "Come on," Jake had said. "We're going out to the Club for lunch."

Don waited for the dark featured man to say something about their phone conversation as they drove, but Jake was uncharacteristically silent. Don got a glimpse of Major Hansard racing by, barely visible above the steering wheel of his Mercedes. "Drives fast," Don remarked.

"That little Englishman." Jake said. "He's the same way about everything. Fast horses, fast cars, fast women."

"At his age? Women?"

"Well, maybe not so much any more. He *is* seventy-five. But it pleases him to have a good-looking girl around. And who knows, maybe he can still get it up."

"Remarkable," Don said, shuddering at the mental image of the randy rooster having sex.

"Money is a great aphrodisiac. It attracts women."

"That's the way you've found it to be, is it?" Don said. He had first-hand knowledge that the absence of money certainly didn't attract them.

Jake glanced over at him. "You need to get laid. It would improve your disposition."

They did not speak the rest of the way. They drove through an older residential section of Velda. Tall trees surrounded well-kept brick houses; wooden fences screened backyards from view. Trees twisted against the wind, which was blowing at a steady clip. The car's heater was on high but Don still shivered.

Jake turned onto Country Club Gulch. They passed the spot where Don had picked up Eugene's truck on Monday. There was a fairly steady stream of cars on the Gulch, most likely Velda's business elite on the way to lunch at the Country Club. Jake pulled into the large parking lot and parked carefully at one end, well away from the pick-ups and Lexus SUVs that filled the parking spaces near the club's entrance.

"No point in inviting somebody to back into my car again," he said. They got out of the car and Jake turned up the collar of his cashmere overcoat. "You don't mind walking?" he asked without waiting for Don to answer.

Don sighed reluctantly. They were a football field length away from the door. He held on to his hat, bent into the cold north wind and followed Jake to the entrance.

The main dining room was at the front of the building, to the left of the entry. The walls were painted a muted cream color and the tables were set with heavy silverware and good looking china, over starched white tablecloths. The large room on the right had a hand-lettered sign that read, "Grill." A bar was visible from the entrance. That room was filled with loud talking men and a few women dressed in their Neiman Marcus best.

Jake walked ahead of him into the dining room. Don followed and looked around. The large room was empty except for a round table in the far corner. Two men sat there. One was Major Hansard. He was tiny, perched on a sort of a high chair; he was staring across the room at a young waitress in a mini-skirt who was carefully setting a table with silverware. The other man was looking at the menu. He looked to be in his early forties, dressed in an out-of-fashion suit with broad stripes, a blue shirt, and green bow tie. His brown hair, flecked with grey, fell carelessly over his forehead as he studied the menu.

31

The waitress dropped a fork and bent down to pick it up, facing the major. Her large breasts did not quite fall out of her low-cut blouse. She smiled fetchingly in the direction of the round table.

"Hello, Major," Jake said to the man in the high chair.

"Join us, Jake," the little man said. It was a command, not an invitation. Jake looked at Don hesitantly.

"Sit, Jake," Hansard repeated. "We have room."

Jake raised his eyebrows and motioned for Don to follow him. They sat down. "Another Scotch?" Jake asked the major.

Hansard nodded absently, still watching the girl. "Yes. No ice." He had a vaguely English accent.

"They know how you like your drink here, Major," Jake said.

He signaled to the girl and pointed at the major's glass. "Beer?" he asked Don.

"Scotch," Don said impudently. "Whatever he's having." He nodded at the major's empty glass. For the first time, the little man looked directly at Don.

"How about you, Tommy?"

The man in the striped suit looked up from the menu. "Well hello, Jake." He spoke with a careless New England accent. Touching his water glass, he said, "This will do, but thanks." He glanced at Don.

"Gentlemen, this is Don Cuinn, a lawyer in my office." He glanced sharply in Don's direction.

He's really unhappy with me, Don thought.

"Cuinn, say hello to Major Hansard, Tommy Crackstone."

Major Hansard glanced at Don, apparently irritated to be interrupted from observing the young waitress as she sashayed to the bar to get their drinks. The major's thinning white hair stood up in careless disarray. "Hmmm, yes, 'lo." He touched Don's outstretched hand with long icy fingers and then turned his attention to brushing breadcrumbs from the front of his heavy Seville Row suit.

Don had spent some slow afternoons at the little museum in the old railroad station down the street from the office, where he had read a lot about the major and his father, Colonel Hansard, the founder of Velda. The Colonel, Cavendish Lytton Hansard, was a corporal in British Army during the Boer War. Afterwards, he became a clerk for an Edinburgh bank. He must have been a good one, because he was sent to Texas by a combine of Scottish bankers who had bought a big piece of the Texas Panhandle from the railroad, which had got the land in part payment for financing the building of the state Capitol Building in Austin.

All that land, Don thought, remembering the enormous spaces he had driven through to get to Velda the first time. Given away to pay for a building. It was a nice building, sure, but a building that housed the likes of former Attorney General Sam Eben Payne. That's what governments do, genetically, I guess; they spend what they don't have on things they don't need.

Scottish bankers had all these land certificates they wanted to convert to cash. They sent Hansard to the Panhandle to survey the land, lay out towns, and sell town lots and farm land. The appraisers whom the bankers had sent to Texas to value the land arrived during one of the

Panhandle's rainy periods. They saw the rolling plains rife with native grasses and proclaimed the Texas Panhandle a farming paradise. Like many appraisers for many banks, they were wrong, but luckily for the Scots, the next drought did not occur until they had cashed out by selling the land.

Hansard founded two towns for his employers, Velda and Antelope City, and with the help of an Illinois medicine show man named Pete Pervoy, successfully sold off thousands of acres of land and most of the town lots. They plastered the American Midwest with posters advertising a new Eden; trainloads of prospective buyers descended on Velda, detraining at the new railroad station, cash in hand, eager to strike it rich.

His employers promoted the Boer War corporal to Colonel to give him status in America. That was around the turn of the last century. Hansard bought land for himself out of his commissions and his bosses let him keep a quarter of the mineral rights. When the Panhandle gas field was discovered, those minerals made the Colonel a very rich man. And of course, he and Pete Pervoy and a couple of others were around to buy out the farmers for a pittance when the droughts came. The big ranches around Velda and Antelope City were put together at that time.

The Colonel said that the rolling prairie reminded him of the South African veldt so he named the town Velda, and he named the streets after himself and his wife. Rosen's law offices were in a building on Cavendish Street. The next street over was Lytton. Those were his surnames. And crossing them were Anne Street and Bulwar and Bowdler. That was the Colonel's wife, Anne Bulwar Bowdler. Her father was a title lawyer and

*abstracter who set up shop in Velda and made his
money selling title abstracts and writing title
opinions for the Colonel's land deals. He became
wealthy, but nothing like the Colonel, and it was
natural that his young daughter and the Colonel
would marry.*

*Faye recounted the town gossip about the
Colonel and his family to Don one slow afternoon.
According to Faye, "Anne died in childbirth, leaving
behind the old Colonel and a runt of a baby,
Cavendish Lytton Hansard II. I understand the old
man was a big brute and he had this tiny child. He
sent the boy back to England for his education.
Eton, Oxford, that sort of thing. When he came
back, the boy moved right in, took over from his
father, booted him out, really, some people say,
forced him to retire to a ranch up in Colorado,
where he died in a few years. Major Hansard has
pretty well had his way in Velda ever since. He's
nobody's fool, even if he's not five feet tall."*

"Don, Tommy's talking to you."

Caught daydreaming he quickly replied,
"Sorry," and looked at the Crackstone heir.

Tommy Crackstone gazed at Don. "I said, it
must be interesting working for Jake." He buttered a
large portion of a dinner roll and took a bite.

Don had never met the heir to the Crackstone
fortune and local vice president of the Crackstone
operation, but of course everyone in Velda knew
who he was. Don recognized the manner. He had
seen it many times with fraternity boys at the
University of Texas, the sense of ease and
entitlement that Don, who had been raised by his
stepmother in a boarding hotel on the west side of
the campus, couldn't acquire in a lifetime. He

35

remembered the advice Wesley Bird had given him. Wesley, Don's friend for many years, until he wasn't a friend any longer, told him, never concede an inch to those bastards. Most of them are soft as butter inside. He wondered if that was true about the Crackstone heir. He said, "Jake is always full of surprises."

"Indeed." Crackstone returned to the menu. "What culinary delight shall we have today, Major?"

"Catfish. Always have the catfish, Tommy." Hansard motioned to the young waitress. She came in a trot to the table. He smiled at her from his perch. The smile looked unnatural. He patted the girl on the arm. "Thank you, Miss Judy." He looked up slyly at Don. "May I suggest the catfish for you as well, Mr. Cuinn?"

"Whatever you say, sir" Don answered, surprised by the major's sudden alertness. He had supposed the major to be senile, but he had obviously been paying close enough attention to remember Don's name while he was observing Miss Judy's charms.

"He knows everything," Faye had warned him once.

The major winked at the girl. "Mr. Cuinn is new to the Club, but he's an up and coming lawyer in Velda." Looking at Don, he addressed the girl again. "No doubt you prefer young men his age. He seems a well-formed young fellow, probably has played sports, a good height, regular features, good head of hair. What do you think?"

Don grimaced and looked down. He could feel the waitress checking him out.

She did a little wiggle. She wasn't just a pretty face. "Oh, Major," she said at last. "You know, I think I prefer more experienced men. Someone, maybe, I don't know, more mature."

The men all roared with laughter and Don did his best to smile. She winked at him when she thought the major wasn't watching. Don wasn't so sure he wasn't watching. In fact, he would have bet that the little man was watching.

Don knew he shouldn't wink back but he did anyway. *Why the hell not?*

Hansard ordered for the table, catfish for Jake, Crackstone and Don and cottage cheese and tomato for himself. The table fell silent.

Jake broke the silence. "Major Hansard gave the land for this club. He arranged the loan to build the clubhouse. He's come here for lunch every day for fifty years."

"Impressive," Don managed to say. He sipped his Scotch and waited. He wanted to say, *who called this meeting?* But he resisted.

They talked about people Don didn't know and the things those people were doing in the oil business and in the cattle business. Finally, the food came and they turned to eating. Crackstone looked at Don. "Cuinn. That's Irish, isn't it?"

Don was surprised. He didn't remember being asked that since high school, when some ill-intentioned classmate tried to tease him about his name. Don was sensitive about the name, as he was, after all, the bastard son of the bastard Marvin Cuinn, who had abandoned his mother. So, he had looked it up.

"Yes, it is. It's Irish."

"All these Gaelic names mean something. What does it mean?"

Don didn't care for the rich man's tone. He took Wesley Bird's advice. "What does Crackstone

37

mean? All these Puritan names mean something, don't they?"

Before he could answer, Jake broke the tension. "Rich. Crackstone means rich."

The others laughed and Don managed to smile. "Cuinn means 'Son of Conn' or 'Son of the Leader.'"

"Ah," Crackstone answered. "And are you that? The son of a leader, I mean?"

Don drained his Scotch. "I couldn't say. I never met the man."

Crackstone eyed him appraisingly. "I like the Irish. My nanny was Irish. A daughter of the Old Sod."

"I think you'll find that we may have Irish names down here, but we're all Texans. My own family, best as I can tell, was Protestants who came to America in the 1700s and moved with the frontier through Carolina, Tennessee, and then Texas in time to fight for independence from Mexico. No memories of the Old Sod."

"Still, an independent lot, I've noticed," Crackstone replied. "It would be a change to have an Irish lawyer."

"I'm sure," Don replied. "I suppose yours have all been Wasps."

"Not all," Crackstone answered.

"Well, would you employ a black lawyer?" Don asked.

"Of course. As long as he was a Harvard man."

Don stared at Crackstone defiantly. *I don't give a shit what you think of me!*

Jake apparently did care, though. "Excuse my young friend's manners, gentlemen."

Crackstone smiled. He brushed crumbs from his tie. "Feisty. I don't mind that."

I'm sitting right here, Don thought.

CHAPTER FIVE

When they were back in Jake's Cadillac, he turned on Don. "You're something else, Cuinn, you know?"

Don reddened. He was still furious at the three men.

Jake slammed his fist against the steering wheel. "I am fed up with you. I give you one last chance and you insult the two most important men in Velda. You snarled at them like a junkyard dog. What the hell's wrong with you?"

Don slumped back in the cold leather seat, shivering. "Why don't you just tell me whatever's on your mind?"

"All right. I'm telling you now. You're fired! Today is your last day. Find somebody else to depress." He started the car and raced down the drive to the exit, throwing gravel up into the wind. "You're an ornery bastard. What makes you act that way?"

"Is it because of the Pervoys?" Don pushed the recline button as far as it would go. He pulled his hat down over his eyes.

"I don't believe I owe you any explanations. But since you ask, yes. Trey doesn't like you."

"I don't even know the man."

"Our most important client and you can't be bothered to get to know him. You're a real piece of work, Don R. Cuinn. A real piece of work. Did I ever tell you how I got the Pervoy account?"

Don didn't reply. *To hell with Pervoy. To hell with the major. And especially, to hell with Tommy Crackstone.*

"I had just gone out on my own, left Salado Jones' firm. I had a few clients, mostly wills, that sort of thing. So one day, George Pervoy II stumbled into my office, drunk and mad as hell. He had run a red light and some ignorant cop gave him a ticket. A ticket! To George Pervoy! Anyway, he was waving the ticket around and I said, 'Give me that thing.' He gave it to me and I said, 'Don't worry about it.' Then I tore it into pieces and tossed it in the trash basket.

"Well, George was impressed. Even drunk, he knew you didn't tear up a ticket. He said, 'What did you do?' I said, 'I know the judge. Don't worry a second about it.' George was tired of being preached at by the Great Salado, and pretty soon I had the reputation of the go-to guy, the lawyer who could fix anything."

"What do you think I did, after George left my office? I'll tell you what I did. I got down on my hands and knees and pulled the pieces of that ticket out of the trash. Then I taped them together and went over to the Justice of the Peace and paid the damn ticket. The best $35.00 I ever spent."

He gunned the engine and roared out of the Country Club parking lot. "But you can't be bothered to know George Pervoy III. To hell with you!"

Don knew he had acted like a horse's ass. He was brittle, almost, but not quite broken, and the only way he knew to deal with the emptiness that pervaded him was to lash back. He had felt loneliness and unhappiness too many times before. *How many losses should a guy be expected to endure?*

The first time, he was a child and his mother had abandoned him to Lena Rothschild, who raised him. He taught himself not to care. Then he met

Wesley Bird, All-American tight end, in a Spanish class at the University of Texas in Austin, and they became like brothers. Wesley introduced him to fun and good times and they promised they would always look after each other, have each other's back. Then Wesley betrayed him, involving him in a political intrigue that nearly ruined his life. He was rescued again, this time by Cecilia, but their short marriage ended in tragedy. *Am I hopeless, destined to be miserable? Who else, but me, would choose this miserable place to be miserable?*

He didn't care anymore. He was a lawyer because of an ad on the wall of the Houston airport. He was in Velda because Drayton Philby had found him a job with Jake. Now he was jobless, broke, with few options.

What am I going to do? Scurry back to Austin with my tail between my legs? I can't do that. What the fuck! Whatever's going to happen, let it happen. It doesn't matter. Nothing ever changes!

Jake was still ranting. "I'll tell Faye to hold your stuff until you decide what you want to do. I'll pay you through the end of the month; settle up on what you're working on. That should get you back to Austin. Tell Drayton I tried my best, will you? It's not my fault."

Jake brought the Caddy to a sharp halt at one of Velda's four red lights. He looked over at Don and took a kinder tone. "Velda's not for you. It's too tough up here. Go back to Austin and find you a left-wing, dope-snortin' girlfriend."

As if that was going to happen! A thought occurred to Don. For a second it roused him out of his funk. He sat up in the seat and took out his cell phone. He found the number of Elmer Thorpe and

speed dialed him in Las Vegas. Elmer was his first
client and he kept his number handy.

Jake gave him a puzzled glance.

Elmer answered the call with his familiar
Panhandle twang. "Elmer Thorpe, wealthy oil man
and devoted husband here."

Lou Jo must be in the room. "Hey, Man. This
is Cuinn. What's going down?"

"Oh, hello, Cuinn. Just settin' here, admiring
my beautiful wife. She just had one of those two
hundred dollar massages, and now she wants to go
to the Strip and hit the tables."

"I won't keep you. You know how you told me
to sell the store?"

He could hear Elmer sipping his drink. "Don't
tell me you sold that piece of shit? What fool did you
find to buy it?"

"Sorry, but no, I haven't sold it."

"Thought that was too good to be true."

"Listen, Elmer. Jake's kicked me out and I'm
setting up practice on my own. I was thinking.
Suppose I rent the store from you. I could hang out
my shingle and live in the back. Would you be
willing for me to do that?"

The old man laughed. "Antelope City has
some pretty strict zoning. Don't know if they'd allow
a lawyer. Whore house yes, but lawyers...don't
know."

"I'll bring in a whore, if you think that would
help."

Don could hear Lou Jo griping in the
background.

"I'm told we've got to go. I tell you what,
Cuinn. I'll give you the damn store. Figure out what
it's worth and pay it out with law work. The way

44

things are going out here, there's probably another divorce in my future." He hung up.

Don pocketed his cell phone and turned to Jake, who was shaking his head. "You're opening up an office in Antelope City, in Elmer's old store on the square?"

"That's the one. A prime location."

"It's not exactly uptown, is it?"

"At least it's away from you."

Jake sighed and punched at his car phone.

Faye's voice came through the speaker. "Yes, Mr. Rosen?"

"Faye, tell Bobby to get the truck and load all of Cuinn's stuff in it. He's moving out to Elmer Thorpe's store."

Don could hear Faye gasp. "He's moving to Antelope City? Why in the world?"

"I guess they don't want him in Austin either."

"But...Antelope City...?"

Jake interrupted. "Just do it," he said wearily.

CHAPTER SIX

J ake let Don out behind the office. Don got in his pick-up, went to his apartment and packed his things. There wasn't much. He hadn't brought much back from Mexico, and most of that was in boxes in Austin.

He decided not to go back to the office. Faye would be sure that Bobby brought him all his stuff. He drove leisurely out the Amarillo highway, ten miles to the metropolis of Antelope City, population 1004, according to the State of Texas road sign. He drove around the town square, looking for any signs of life. The Panhandle wind had blown trash against the statue of an antelope that adorned the square. The courthouse would have been on that square if Velda had not stolen the courthouse away in the 1920s. Someone had tried to clean the graffiti off the statue but Don could still make out "Antelope Sucks" sprayed in red on the statue's rump. Its sharp horns faced north and its ass faced south, where Don would see it every morning. *That works.*

Elmer's store was on the south side of the square. The door was padlocked. An R C Cola sign hung in one dirty window. The metal shutters were closed. Behind the store, oil well pump jacks nodded up and down sleepily.

The first time he met the Thorpes, Don had only been in Velda a week and Jake was in Dallas. Don could hear the man and woman when they got off the elevator.

"Just shut up," the man said, his voice High Plains flat and resigned.

47

The reply had the demanding nasal edginess of a big-haired Panhandle girl. "You tell me to shut up once more and you'll wish you hadn't, I swear to God."

Faye ushered them into his office, nodded grimly at Don and closed the door behind her.

They settled uneasily onto the wood chairs in front of Don's uncluttered oak desk. The man wore his going-to-town outfit, a stiffly starched white dress shirt with pearl buttons and a pair of ironed jeans. He was average height; an athletic build had given way to late middle age. Whiskey lines crossed his large nose. He held his Stetson in his rough hands, twirling it with arthritic fingers. He looked at Don with faded blue eyes. "I'm Elmer Thorpe. This here..." He nodded toward the woman. "This here is my wife Lou Jo. I hope soon to say, my ex-wife."

The woman snorted. "You hope. I pray!" She appeared to be younger than her husband, bone thin, all sharp elbows and knees, hair dyed as black as the law would allow, blue mascara outlining her darting hazel eyes, thin lips outlined with bright red lipstick. She wore a dazzling blue dress with puffy sleeves and sensible shoes. A matching blue bow perched atop her bee-hive.

"You ain't Rosen." Elmer looked around the office, as if he expected to find Jake hiding in a corner.

"Excuse me?"

"Lawyer Jake. Is he here?"

"Mr. Rosen is in court in Dallas. I'm his associate, Don Cuinn. Maybe I can help you?"

Elmer stared appraisingly at Cuinn. "You're pretty young. What do you think, Lou Jo?"

"I guess if he says he's a lawyer, he probably is one. He can't be any worse than the last one." She shifted her weight. "You're paying. You decide."

Elmer grumbled. "I paid the last time. Seems like you ought to pay for something."

Lou Jo ignored that. "Do you do divorces?"

Cuinn nodded, he hoped not too eagerly. A divorce! "Of course. You folks want a divorce?"

"I guess you could call it a re-divorce," Elmer said.

"A what?"

"A re-divorce. Five years ago we got divorced, then three years after that we got re-married. Now we want to get re-divorced."

"Can I ask why?"

"Why what?" Elmer asked.

"Why do you want to get, uh, re-divorced?"

Elmer eyed him suspiciously. "Don't see how that's any of your business."

"Oh, Elmer," Lou Jo interrupted, turning to Don. "It's Antelope City. When we bought the store, Elmer promised me one day we'd sell it and move someplace that has a picture show."

"Antelope City has a picture show," Elmer asserted.

Lou Jo disagreed, the blue bow bobbing. "Antelope City does not either have a picture show. Just because that drive-in's screen is still out in that pasture, it definitely does not count as a picture show if they never show anything." She returned her attention to Don. "It's been shut down for fifteen years."

She took a deep breath. "When we got re-married, he promised me again. We started selling the liquor, the only liquor store in driving distance of Velda, which is dry, you know."

"Yes, I know." Don had been in Thorpe's store himself, and now he recalled the skinny woman behind the counter.

He looked down at his blank legal pad. "About the divorce. There's an irreconcilable difference about moving to a larger city?"

"It is not irreconcilable. It could be reconciled in a second. All he has to do is sell the business and move," she said.

"It ain't the time to move. When the time comes, it will come," Elmer replied.

Lou Jo pressed her lips tightly. "See? He's so stubborn. He'll never leave Antelope City. I'm moving to Amarillo and I want a divorce and my half of everything."

Don explained that he could only represent one of them, and after ten minutes of bickering, the couple decided Elmer would be his client. Don called Wiley Franklin, the only lawyer in town making less money than Don; Wiley eagerly took Lou Jo on. Too eagerly, Don thought, making meaningless changes in his and Faye's divorce petition, and marking up the property settlement.

And so they divorced. Elmer got the store and the land around it; Lou Jo got the cash they had on deposit in the Bank of Velda. That would support her just fine in Amarillo, she said.

"I miss that bony-ass," Elmer confessed to Don when he came to Velda to pay his bill. He pulled out a chrome Zippo and lit a cigarette. "But she'll be back, soon as she runs out of money."

"There's still no picture show in Antelope City." Don pushed a saucer in front of Elmer for an ashtray.

"She'll be back."

50

Elmer knew everybody in the county, and his friends started showing up in Don's office with their speeding tickets and workers' compensation claims, some wills, and their own divorces. Whenever a new client showed up, Don made a point of driving to Antelope City to thank Elmer and take him a carton of cigarettes. After one especially nice referral he went out to Antelope City only to be met by Lou Jo.

"You're back? That was quick."

Lou Jo opened a beer for Don and then decided to have one herself. "I'll tell you, Cuinn. Amarillo is God-awful expensive."

"Did you enjoy the picture show?"

She brushed the bottle caps into a trashcan. "They do not make moving pictures like they used to."

Three months later, Cuinn got an invitation to the wedding.

Lou Jo returned to Antelope City in time for one of the periodic upswings in the oil business. Don negotiated the lease with Conoco on Elmer's old family place, six hundred and forty acres south of Antelope City. The next time Don was there, pump jacks had sprouted up all over and Elmer was flipping through his royalty checks. He looked up at Don through his rheumy eyes. "This ain't good, ain't good a'tall."

Don got himself a beer. "You don't like being rich?"

"Hell, yes, I like it. The problem is Lou Jo."

"Picture show?"

"You got it. She's after me to move. She's upgraded from Amarillo. Now it's Las Vegas. She buys those magazines and reads me the shows in Las Vegas. She's gone on the damn Internet,

51

teaching herself to play blackjack. Night and day,
it's Vegas this, Vegas that." He frowned. "I'm sick to
death of hearing about Vegas."

The Texas Rangers were losing to the
Yankees on Elmer's big screen TV. Elmer stared at
the girls playing beach volleyball in the
commercial. The back door was open. The sun
reflected off the green and white pump jacks.

"What are you going to do?" Don asked.

"She owns half of all them, didn't you say?"
Elmer pointed at the pump jacks.

"I believe that's right. Community property."

"Shit," the old man sighed. "We should have
stayed re-divorced."

"It would seem so."

The next time Don heard from Elmer was by
United States mail. The letter was scrawled on a
piece of ruled tablet paper:

Lou Jo left. Says she ain't coming back, and
this time I guess she means it. Here's the key to the
store. Take anything you want and sell the rest.
Give the money to the Preservation Society to clean
up that statue. I'll be in Vegas, taking in a show
with Mrs. Elmer Thorpe.

Don unlocked the door and gave it a strong push. He
had forgotten in how bad a mess the Thorpes had
left the place; old cartons of empty bottles, piles of
newspapers, a partially cleaned-out cooler. Thank
God he'd never got around to having the utilities
turned off. Shivering from the cold, he switched on
the ancient gas furnace and it cranked up with a
groan. He found some beer left behind in the cooler.
He sat at Elmer's place at the counter and tried to
decide where to start. He rang up "No Sale" on the
old fashioned cash register.

Surprisingly, the living quarters at the rear of the store were almost clean. Running in the cold from car to store, he propped the door open with a branding iron that Elmer had left. The wind worked at the old door, trying to blow it shut, but Don managed to pile everything in the corner of the bedroom except for his shaving kit, which he hung on a rusty hook next to the bathroom sink. He brushed his teeth and took two aspirin, remade the bed with a pair of fresh sheets and spread a blanket on top.

He had just gone to sleep when he heard someone rattle the front door. *Go away.*

"Cuinn? Lawyer Cuinn? Are you in there?" It was Eugene. It was pitch dark outside.

"Jesus Christ," he muttered. He pulled on his pants and staggered to the front door. He opened the door and motioned for the rangy rancher to come in.

Eugene nodded and looked around. "Ginelle said I needed a lawyer." He brushed the debris off one of the stools and sat down. He lit a cigarette and looked around again. "You know, this looks like a mess, even to me."

"What do you want, Eugene? Another moving violation?"

"Lawyer Jake's my moving violation lawyer." He looked longingly at the cooler.

Don poked around and finally found two beers in the cooler. He opened them and handed one to Eugene, who was rubbing his eyes sleepily.

"Why are you here, Eugene?"

"I told you. Ginelle said I needed a lawyer."

Don sipped the cold beer. He had almost lost his patience. "You have a lawyer, Eugene. Jake

Rosen is your family's lawyer. Go wake him up at midnight."

The cowboy took off his hat and extracted a legal size envelope, folded in half. He put it on the counter and looked at it warily. "These papers. Trey says Lawyer Jake drew them up and wants me to sign them. Ginelle reads all the time, and she can't tell what they mean. She and me want you to tell us what they mean."

Don opened the envelope and pulled out the contents. He was looking at a document entitled: *Waiver and Clarification of Terms of Trust Agreement.* "Jake sent you these?"

"Trey brought them over hisself."

"Did Trey say what they were?"

Eugene lit another cigarette. "He said it was to clear up something, something about clearing up."

"A clarification? Is that what he said?"

"That's it. A clarification, so that I can keep getting my trust check every month."

Don riffled through the papers. "Did Trey say that?"

"He did. Like I said, Trey brought them to the house and wanted to take me into town so I could sign the papers and swear to them." He found himself another beer, not asking or offering one to Don. "Hell, I'd just got home from town. I had a load of semen to deal with. I wasn't going to turn around and go back to town."

They stared at the papers silently. Don still wasn't awake. He waited. "And then . . . ?"

"And then, Troy said that I needed to go to town and sign the papers if I wanted to keep my monthly trust checks coming. 'Keep those checks coming' is what he said."

54

"What did you tell him?"

"That I was too busy. That I'd do it the next day. After he finally left, Ginelle and I talked about it and we called Miss Faye and asked her what we should do. She said I needed my own lawyer. She said you and Lawyer Jake had split the blanket, and I should come out here and see you."

Jake's going to love this. His own secretary sending his best client's brother to the lawyer he just fired. For the first time in a long time, he almost felt good, almost felt normal. He actually laughed. "Leave them with me, Eugene. I'll look at them right away."

"What do I tell Trey?"

"Tell him you're having your own lawyer look them over. If he wants to know who, tell him you found an out-of-town lawyer to advise you."

Eugene took a long draw on his cigarette. "You're out of town all right. You're damned near out of this world." He walked over to the pile of junk that took up half of the old store. "What's all this?"

Don shrugged. "Stuff Elmer never threw away. I guess it belongs to me now. Mine to haul away."

Eugene picked up a tire tool. "Do you want this?"

"Take it. It's yours. I might ought to keep it though. I may need it to bash Jake over the head when he comes complaining I've stolen his client."

Eugene bristled. "Stoled? You never stoled me. I'm a free man, ain't I? Reckon I can have any lawyer I want, can't I?"

"I imagine so." He decided to have another beer himself. Eugene joined him, then picked through the pile of junk, turning over the old beer signs and advertising posters.

55

"I suspect Ginelle's cousin Raynelle in Amarillo would buy this off of you, seeing how she's in the collectables business."

"Send her over. I was just going to throw it all out."

"No. Don't do that." Eugene picked up a beer bottle. "Look here. People pay for old Jax beer bottles." He was acting like he might stay a while.

The cowboy reached into his jean pocket. "Before I forget, Ginelle told me to give you this." He handed Don a folded check.

The check was on the Bank of Velda for five thousand dollars. Surprised, he looked up at Eugene. "No call for this, Eugene. Wait and see what I do for you."

"No, no sir. It's for you. On account, Ginelle said." He struggled for the word. "What do you call it, a re-tender?"

"A retainer?"

"That's the one. You're my lawyer, right? That check seals the deal."

"I'll do what I can, Eugene. In the meantime, don't sign anything."

"Not 'til my lawyer says to, right?

"Exactly right. Your out-of-town lawyer."

CHAPTER SEVEN

Don woke with a six-beer hangover. The old heater spewed out warm air through what had to be a filthy filter and the blowing air stirred up dust from everywhere. The wind howled across the square, rattling the metal shutters. Something banged somewhere.

After Eugene left, Don had stayed up reading the documents, trying to decipher Jake's convoluted prose. He was confident that Jake had written it himself. If Faye had drafted it, it would be a lot easier to understand. *Jake didn't want it to be easy to understand, did he?* Cutting through the verbiage, it seemed to be an agreement that the Pervoy Family Trust granted the trustee the right to sell water rights as well as the oil and gas rights.

What's that all about? Don wondered. *Some byzantine tax scheme that Jake's tax counsel had dreamed up?* He wasn't exactly sure what Jake was getting at, but he was pretty sure it wasn't intended to benefit Don's new client. He needed to call Eugene, discuss this with him, before he forgot and signed the damn papers.

The shower produced hot water. *Thank God.* He made coffee from the half-empty can the Thorpes had left behind. It was not good coffee, but it was hot. He dried off with one of his clean towels, brushed his teeth, ran the towel over his damp hair and pulled on a clean dress shirt and pair of jeans and reached Eugene on the cowboy's cell phone.

"Eugene," he asked loudly, "has anybody said anything to you about the Pervoy Family Trust?"

"Hell, no. What about it?"

"If I understand this right, they want all the beneficiaries to agree that the trustee can sell the water rights."

"Water rights, did you say? Why?"

"That I can't tell you. Just be sure you don't sign anything until we find out why. And would you ask Ginelle to call her cousin and have her come look at Elmer's junk pile. I'd like to get rid of that stuff."

"That matter is already under way," Eugene answered.

"Just tell her not to get here before eight a.m., all right?"

"Lawyers," he heard Eugene mutter before he hung up the phone.

He needed food. He decided to drive into Velda, stock up and put Eugene's check in the bank. See if it cleared. Then he decided against going to the bank. Jake would know in ten minutes if Don deposited a Pervoy check in the bank. He needed time before that happened. But he did need food. And more beer.

He drove out the Loop to the Wal-Mart on the northwest side of Velda. He had been on the Loop before, of course, but he had not paid much attention. This morning the sun reflected off the row of low sheds in the distance. They were the only structures visible on the large tract of land alongside the highway. It was protected by a twelve foot fence with barbed wire on the top. He made a mental note to find out what was out there. He knew it was government land, something called Evergreen, but that was all he knew.

He was going eighty when he rounded a curve. A dozen young women stood in the middle of the road carrying picket signs. He threw on his brakes and barely missed them. Shaken, he coasted to a stop. They surrounded his car, shouting.

He rolled down the window. A college-age woman stuck her head inside the window. She had a wool cap pulled down over her ears and a parka and scarf. Her eyes were watering and her nose was running. "Hi," she said brightly. She pointed at the entrance behind her, "You can't go in the Evergreen plant today. We're picketing it."

The plant had a guardhouse and double gates. Don could see a soldier with a rifle inside the guardhouse. "I'd hate to cross a picket line. I'll just go on down the road."

"He's not going in!" the girl yelled at the others, and they started cheering. "Strontium Kills! Cesium Go Away! No More Nukes! No More Nukes! No More Nukes!"

Don could make out the guard on his phone. A sign on the gate read: "United States Department of Energy Facility." And below that, in red letters and the picture of a soldier holding a rifle: "Trespassers Will Be Shot."

Don pointed at the guard and said, "I think he's calling for reinforcements."

"We're not moving. This place is a hazard to the entire nation."

"They probably don't look kindly on you trying to block the entrance to a U.S. government facility."

"They'll have to arrest us, because we're not moving." She turned to the others. "No More Nukes!" The others joined in the shout. "No More Nukes! No More Nukes!"

Looking in his rear view mirror, Don saw the entire Velda County anti-terrorist task force, all three officers, plus a convoy of highway patrolmen descending on the twelve college students, sirens blaring. At the same time from inside the facility, Jeeps and trucks manned with troops arrived at the gate. He heard the whumping sound of a helicopter and in a second it was hovering over the protesters, the blades blowing the north wind in all directions. The acrid smell of fuel oil drifted over the entire scene.

The peace officers surrounded the protesters and a skinny highway patrolman with a megaphone ordered them to disperse. Their replies of "Fascists" and "Free Speech!" were drowned out by the helicopter.

Talk about overkill. Don pulled out a business card, scratched out the address and wrote in "On the Square, Antelope City, Texas." He called the girl back to his car and handed it to her. "You're probably going to need a lawyer. If you do, call me."

She took the card, held it between her teeth and pulled off a mitten. She unzipped her parka and stuffed his card down the front of her blouse. She winked at Don. "I'm Maggie Shirls. I may call you anyway."

One of the highway patrolmen ordered him out of his car, but he was rescued by Boom Gordon. "What in the world are you doing out here, Cuinn? Not protesting, I hope."

"I live in Antelope City now, Boom. I was on my way to get some eggs and milk."

"Right answer," Boom replied with a wink that said he did not believe a word of it. "He's O.K., Sharkey," he said to the highway patrolman. "Just an ambulance chaser out cruising for business."

"Well tell him to cruise somewhere else, will you?"

60

"You heard the man. On your way, Counselor," Boom said, patting the side of Don's car with a beefy fist.

As he put the car in gear he called to Boom. "It looks like Miz Bessie's going to have company for lunch. She'd better put on a big pot of stew. Those girls will be awfully hungry."

The Wal-Mart parking lot was empty except for a couple of pick-up trucks. A large family spilled out of the store, the little ones yelling and playing tag. He stopped in a corner of the football size parking lot, away from the toddlers and thought about Eugene. *Of course. Faye.* He dialed her on his cell phone and heard her familiar voice on the line.

"Rosen Law Office."

"Not 'Rosen and Associates', Faye?"

"Oh, hello, Mr. Cuinn. Are you getting settled?"

"Yes I am. In fact, my first client was on the porch last night, banging on the door."

She laughed. "I'm surprised Eugene was up after sundown."

Don shooed away four little kids who wanted to climb in the back of his truck. "Faye, let me ask you something. Now that Eugene's my client . . ."

"Can I send you the Pervoy Family Trust? I'm sure Mr. Eugene Pervoy in entitled to a copy of his family trust. In fact, I have it right here." He heard efficient keyboarding. "There. It's on its way to your tablet."

"You're wonderful, Faye. Remind me to send you some flowers."

"Don't waste your retainer money on me, Mr. Cuinn. Eugene brought the check, I hope?"

61

Don patted his coat pocket. "I have it right here."

"Well, I'd suggest you open a bank account in Amarillo, some nice big national bank with strict rules about customer privacy."

Don grinned. "You read my mind. Well, thanks again. Gotta go get some groceries."

"Good luck, Mr. Cuinn. Eugene and his family deserve a good lawyer, and as I told him, you are a very good lawyer." She lowered her voice. "One more thing, I included with the trust an opinion that Mr. Rosen got from Filbert and Jacama, down in Dallas. The trust attorneys? The Pervoys paid for it, so I'm sure Mr. Rosen would want Eugene to have it."

"I'm sure, Faye. But we won't bother him with that right now, as busy as he is."

"You be careful, Mr. Cuinn. And good day to you."

CHAPTER EIGHT

H e decided to drive to Amarillo and open that bank account. It was late afternoon before he got back to Antelope City.

Circling the square, he saw a familiar skinny figure on the front porch, broom in hand. *Jesus, Faye, you're something else,* he thought. He parked his truck and got out. "Faye?" he called. "What in the world are you doing?"

The woman turned to face him and to his surprise, it was not Faye. She looked like Faye, except she wore much more make-up and sported a big hair, hair-do.

"Hello?" he said, as he recovered from his surprise.

She stopped sweeping and extended a bony hand. "You have to be Mr. Cuinn. I'm Maye Martin, Faye's sister."

He shook her hand. "Faye's sister?"

"Her twin sister, to be exact." She went back to her sweeping. "Faye told me you needed help out here, but I never had any idea." She wiped her face with a purple bandana. "But we'll make a law office out of this place yet."

The store door was open. "How did you get in?"

"Walked in," she answered. "You really need to lock up when you leave. Not to worry, I've got the locksmith coming over from Amarillo in the morning to change the locks. Come inside. I need to ask you where you want the conference table."

She held the screen open and he followed her in. "What conference table?"

"Well, I never saw a law office without a conference table, and I worked in the biggest law firm in Amarillo. Until I retired. Never mind. If you don't know, I'll work it out."

"What conference table?" he repeated.

"Mr. Rosen has a warehouse full of office furniture, desks and book cases, things he got tired of. Faye sent out what she thought we would need."

"We?"

"I told Faye I would come over here and help you get set up. I'll stay as long as you need me."

He looked around. The place had been cleaned out. A secretary's desk and a row of file cabinets had been installed behind Elmer's counter. The store shelves and signs and the rest of Elmer's collectables were piled neatly outside the back door. Several wooden chairs and a scarred coffee table were in their place. The door to the side room, Elmer Thorpe's office, was open. There was Don's desk, straight from his office at Rosen's. "You did all this?"

"I had some help, Bobby McCathey and a boy he brought." She looked around. "There's still a lot to do. I thought we might put the conference table in the old store room, where the freezer was?"

"Where is the freezer? I could use a beer."

"It's out back, in the shed. I saved the old signs, the cow bell, stuff like that. They're probably worth something."

"Eugene Pervoy's wife's cousin is coming to take a look, I think."

She shook her head disapprovingly. "That Raynelle Gibson? You leave that little tramp to me. I'll have to watch her like a hawk or she'll steal us blind."

"I was going to throw it all out . . ."

64

Maye clucked her disapproval again. "Nobody's ever accused lawyers of being good businessmen." She sighed heavily and started sweeping some more. "That's what you have me for, I guess."

"I guess," Don agreed. He watched her empty her dust pan in the big trash can out back. "This is amazing. Does Jake know all his stuff is here?"

"I imagine Faye will tell him if she thinks he needs to know."

"Wait right here," he said. "I need to put these groceries away. Would you like a beer?"

"No, thank you. You should know, Mr. Cuinn, that unlike my sister, I do use alcohol. But never during office hours. I could use a Coca Cola though. I seem to have worked up a thirst."

When he returned with a beer and a Coke, Maye was sitting at the desk behind the counter, entering a list on a computer terminal.

"Jesus," he said, handing her the Coke and looking over her shoulder. "We got a computer from Jake too?"

She nodded and then said briskly, "We need to get the phone and Internet hooked up. We need to install accounting software. I think we can use the program I put in at the law firm." She looked up at him sharply. "In Amarillo? Thompson, Fite? The biggest firm in town? I was their administrative manager."

"Well, gee, Faye, I mean Maye, this is wonderful, but I can't afford you."

"Faye says you got a retainer check this morning, Hand it over. I'll open accounts for you in Amarillo tomorrow."

"I did that this morning." He handed her the deposit slip.

65

"Oh well. No, Mr. Cuinn. That money needs to go into your client account. It's a retainer. You can transfer it to the firm's account as you earn it. Do you understand?"

"I'm afraid they didn't teach law office management at my law school."

"Faye sent an accounting for the cases you were working on with Mr. Rosen, along with a check. Look at it and see if it's right."

He looked at the statement and the check. "God, Jake was generous. I never expected that much." Maye stared at him. "Oh, I see. Another of Faye's acts of kindness."

"She really likes you, Mr. Cuinn. Be sure you repay her confidence in you."

He didn't answer. He wasn't sure if he liked where this conversation was going. He did not want to feel indebted to anyone, not even Faye. "I'll study it carefully and be sure it's not too much," he said.

"We can survive on that for a little while," Maye said. "Endorse it and I'll deposit it in the morning, open the trust account, and take care of other housekeeping in Amarillo. I imagine we need to get your hourly rate up." She looked him over closely. "You do have other clients?"

Don sat down beside her desk. He took a swig of the Coors. "Not really. A few of Elmer's Thorpe's relatives." His cell phone rang. "Maybe that's a client now."

"Let us devoutly hope," the skinny woman replied, typing furiously at her computer terminal.

It was Boom. "I've got some college girls down here at the jail. One of them has your card. Are you going to come get them?"

"Have they been charged?"

66

"No. Talk to the D.A. If he agrees and you promise to get them out of town and keep them out, I'll release them to your custody. I'm keeping their weed."

"Jesus. Really?"

Richard Cator had not heard that Don was no longer associated with the Rosen Law Firm and Don did not break the news to him.

"So let me get this straight," the District Attorney said. "You want me to *not* file charges on some trespassers at the Evergreen Plant gate, even though the Panhandle Anti-Terrorism Task Force arrested them and we have them here in the Velda County jail?"

"They're just college students, Richard, on a lark. A college deal. Free Speech. First Amendment. Choose a reason. Just let them go. Plus they didn't trespass. They were in the road."

"They were blocking the entrance to a restricted government facility, and that's just as bad."

"So what is Evergreen, anyway? Some nuclear facility, isn't it?"

"You live in Velda and that's all you know about Evergreen?"

"Color me dumb."

Cator shook his head. "Evergreen was the assembly plant for all of the country's nuclear weapons. Then when we started playing footsie with the Russians, we agreed to stop making bombs and start disassembling them. You do remember that?"

"Vaguely."

"Well, Evergreen is where the bombs are being taken apart."

"Let me get this straight. We're not making the bombs anymore; we're unmaking them. Why would my new clients object to that?"

"Hell, I don't know. Ask them. I will say this. Evergreen has always been on the protest circuit for all the tree-huggers and greenies. They didn't like it when they were making the bombs and now they don't like the way they're handling the plutonium and whatever else they salvage when they decommission the weapons. Believe me, if the government did everything they're asking for, it wouldn't make any difference. They'd still be out there, shaking their cute little butts and feeling good about being against the government."

"In other words, they're misguided kids."

Cator drummed his fingers on his desk. "Jake wants this?"

Don did not hesitate. "Of course."

"O.K. Get them out of the county, out of the Northern District of Texas, before the D. of J. comes down on my butt."

Don stood. "I'm on it. Thanks very much, Richard."

"Give Jake a message for me, will you? Tell him that Kelley's probably going to retire. Whether he does or not, I'm going to be running for District Judge. That's an expensive race."

"I'll be sure to mention it the next time we speak."

Don had parked in the handicapped spot in front of the courthouse. He could hear the giggles before he got to the Gordons' apartment. He opened the door and went inside. Two of the girls were kneeling on the floor beside Miz Bessie, giving her a manicure. The others were sitting around Boom, laughing at something he had just said. They looked up when Don entered.

"Mr. Cuinn, Attorney at Law!" Maggie Shirls shouted. "Go away! We don't want to leave. We love it here!"

The others joined in, laughing. One said, "Come back later. We're going to give the Sheriff a haircut."

Boom stirred himself out of his recliner. "Next time maybe. No. I don't mean that. Don't let there ever be a next time, you hear? Cuinn, get these trouble-makers out of my county."

The girls huddled around Boom and his wife, hugging them. Don finally loaded them into his pick-up. The ones in the back waved and threw kisses to the few bemused bystanders outside the courthouse. He needed to get them out of town as soon as possible.

Don delivered the girls to the two minibuses they had left a short distance from the Evergreen plant entrance. The buses were decorated with peace symbols and other graffiti. The terrorism task force had apparently adjourned to the Greeks for lunch. "Get out of here fast," he told them. "Don't go back to Amarillo. There's trouble there. Go straight north, out of Texas just as fast as you can." He paused and then added. "Without getting a speeding ticket, for Christ's sake."

Maggie Shirls gave him a kiss on the lips and the others all gave him hugs. He finally herded them into the minibuses and watched them take off to Oklahoma, and he hoped, to freedom. He did not feel bad about these Greenies escaping justice.

CHAPTER NINE

A norther had blown through and the cloudless sky was a startling blue color. The arroyos and breaks to the north were bathed in sunlight, alternating with shadows from the large cottonwood trees that ringed Thorpe's store. There was something else unusual and it took Don a minute to realize what it was. The wind had stopped and there was only a light breeze from the north. It was in fact a gloriously beautiful day. *No, it's not,* he told himself.

It was quiet enough they could hear the green pick-up truck stop in front of the store. Maye spotted it first, as she did most things. "Client coming," she said over her shoulder to Don.

He had spent the last few days handling assorted legal problems for some of his old clients, mostly Thorpe relatives, who wandered around the store in a daze, as if they expected Elmer to come out of a dark corner and tell them they were in the right place. He finally had time to study the Pervoy documents, but now he closed his tablet and waited expectantly. He hoped he look like a prosperous lawyer.

A skinny man about fifty, wearing a shiny polyester white shirt, a floral tie and wrinkled dress pants peered through the distorted glass pane in the front door. He looked up at Don's newly painted sign, looked down at papers in his hand, and came inside. He nodded at Maye through thick gold-framed glasses.

"Is this Elmer Thorpe's place?"

"No sir, it is not," Maye answered with a disappointed frown. She was hoping for a paying client. "These are the law offices of Don R. Cuinn.

"I see," the man answered. "Someone told me Mr. Thorpe might have moved out to Las Vegas or somewhere, with his wife?"

Maye did not answer. She did not give out information. She took in information.

"Do you know how I might reach him?"

She still did not answer. Don could see that Maye didn't know if Elmer Thorpe wanted to be reached or not and meanwhile she was not having any of the stranger. *This could go on all day.* He got to his feet and went into the waiting room. "I'm Don Cuinn, Elmer Thorpe's lawyer. Can I help you?"

"My name's Hoppy Johnson," the thin man said. "I need to talk to Mr. Thorpe."

"What's this about?" Don said.

"I'm a landman." Hoppy cleared his throat and patted his shirt pocket.

He wishes he had a cigarette, Don thought. "Light up if you want to."

He watched Hoppy light a cigarette. The skinny landman took a long drag. "I have a proposal for Mr. Thorpe."

"I handle all of Mr. Thorpe's oil and gas matters. Tell me what you've got." He led Hoppy into the former storeroom and they settled around the old conference table. Maye brought them both a coffee and set an ashtray in front of the landman. She left the room and shut the door behind her. *Just like a real law office.*

Hoppy took a term sheet out of his coat pocket and laid it on the table in front of Don. "I represent a client who wants to buy Mr. Thorpe's water rights."

Water rights. What a small world. "What company? And did you say buy? Not lease?"

"Yes, they want to buy his water rights. For a very generous price."

Don picked up the term sheet and tried not to let his surprise show. *A really generous price.* "What company, did you say?"

"It's a conservancy, founded by a couple of prominent local men. They believe the water rights ought to stay in local hands and they're willing to pay a lot to see that they do."

Don stared at the term sheet. "I have to confess, I'm a little out of my depth here. I've never done a water deal before."

"Me neither." Hoppy took another long drag and ground the butt into the ashtray. "But I will tell you this. This offer is legit. The money's there."

"You say they want the water rights to stay in local hands. What do you mean by that?"

"There's a company, out of Fort Worth, that's trying to lease up the water rights, ship the water downstate. My clients don't want that to happen."

"Is that Sawbucks Banjo? I read something about that."

"You'll hear a lot more about it. He's making a big land play all over the county, leasing water rights. He wants to build a pipeline all the way to Dallas-Fort Worth, take Velda's water and sell it down there."

"And your clients, these local investors who are opposed to that, are just civic-minded?" He held up the term sheet. "Extremely civic-minded."

Hoppy smiled. "Well, it sure seems so. They're reputable. As I said, the money's there. I wouldn't be here if they weren't on the up and up."

Don stood up. "Leave me your number. I'll get hold of Elmer and talk to him about it."

He stood by Maye, watching the landman drive away. "I need to talk to Elmer Thorpe right away."

Elmer answered on the first ring. "I see it's you again, Cuinn. What is it this time? You want to give the store back?"

"I do not. This place is a well-oiled legal machine. But there is some news. There's an outfit that wants to buy your water rights."

"Hell, that's not news. I've already leased my water rights."

"Leased them? Without talking to me? Who to?"

"I sent you the papers. I made a deal with Sawbucks."

Don remembered the envelope on the top of the stack of mail in his office at Jake's. It seemed like a lifetime. "Maye," he yelled. "Did Faye send over my mail?"

Maye sashayed into his office and laid the envelope on his desk. "Is this what you're looking for?"

He took the envelope and nodded his thanks. Maye had slit it open. He shook the contents onto his desk. "Here it is, Elmer. Let me look at it and I'll call you back in a minute."

"Well, hurry up. We're on our way to see Wayne Newton."

To his relief, Don found that all Elmer had done so far was agree with a Banjo landman to lease his water rights. The papers included a lease and a sight draft for Thorpe to present to the Bank of Amarillo. If and when Banjo's company told the bank to pay the draft, it would deliver the lease to

Banjo and the purchase money to the Thorpes. Fortunately, Elmer had sent the papers for Don to look over. *There is no deal.*

Don called Elmer back at once. "Listen, Elmer. I'm going to hold onto these papers. I don't want you to sign them until we can review this other deal. It's a cash deal, a lot of cash. Sawbucks is paying isn't much of anything. You might get something if his water deal goes through. This other deal is cash right now, but they will own your water. We need to look at it closely."

"Jesus. I could use cash!" He could hear the old man clink the ice in his glass. "Some more whiskey, woman."

"I imagine you'll hear from Banjo's landman pretty soon. If you do, just refer him to me."

The runway lights flashed on and the Twin Beech Baron landed about halfway down the hardpack landing strip. The pilot cut the engines and the plane coasted silently to the metal hanger. All the lights went off. Two black Cadillac SUVs were waiting in the dark.

A man opened the exit door from inside the plane. He reached around and fastened the door against the fuselage. He folded down the gangway and motioned to the men in the SUVs. Four men got out of the Cadillacs and went to the gangway. No one spoke. The man inside handed four suitcases down to the men. They hoisted them in their arms and deposited them in the back of the SUVs. The transfer took less than ten minutes. When they were done, the man in the plane hopped down and got into one of the SUVs. They drove off quietly, no lights visible.

The pilot of the plane started one engine and maneuvered it into the hanger. All went quiet. He closed the hanger door, got into a pick-up parked beside the hanger and drove away.

CHAPTER TEN

Maye handed Don the phone. "It's Mr. Rosen," she mouthed.

Uh oh.

"Cuinn my friend, rhymes with sin," he heard Jake say. "I hope you're enjoying that extravagant check my incompetent office manager sent you."

"You'll have to take that up with her, I guess. It looked all right to me."

"Yeah, it would. She may think I don't know what's going on, but my *tatteh* ran a dry goods store in Childress and he taught me well. I know where every penny comes from and where it goes. She paid you way too much."

"Like I said . . ." Don motioned to Maye for a cup of coffee, which appeared before Jake continued.

"So be it. She works for me. It was worth it to get rid of you."

"I'm pleased you feel that way, Jake."

He heard papers shuffling on the other end of the line. Jake said, "You don't happen to be the out-of-town lawyer that represents Eugene Pervoy, do you?"

"Why do you ask?"

"Because if you are, you would be well advised to have him sign the papers his brother gave him. We need those papers signed right away. The hearing before Judge Kelley is next week."

"I doubt that Eugene will be signing any papers that soon."

"So he is your client. Too bad. I was going to get you appointed by the judge to represent all the unknown and unborn heirs. Nice fee for doing nothing."

"I'm sure you can find someone to do that. But before Eugene signs anything, you and I need to meet. I want to understand what's going on."

"Sure, we can meet. But it's pretty clear, isn't it? The trust allows the trustee to sell the water rights. Everyone agrees to that. We just need a declaratory judgment to that effect."

"Hmm. If it's so clear, why the declaratory judgment?"

"Oh, you know. Legal technicality. Just to clear the record. You understand that, I'm sure."

"Well, I have to protect my client. You understand that, I'm sure."

"The hell you say. You want to screw with me, after I've been so generous to you?"

"Don't threaten me, Jake. You can have your check back." He looked up at Maye, who shook her head violently. He grinned.

"I don't want the check back. I want Eugene's signature on those papers."

Don waited; said nothing.

"All right, all right. Come on down, I'll walk you through it, make it plain enough so even a graduate of the Jeff Davis Law School can understand it."

Don made an OK signal to Maye. "I'm pretty busy, Jake. Why don't you come out here?"

"You horse's ass. All right. I'll be there in thirty minutes."

"No can do, Jake. Big client conference." He needed time to look over the papers again. Besides, this was fun. "Make it about three. I think I'm free then."

"One more thing," Jake said. "Don't you ever use my name when you're plea bargaining with the district attorney or anyone else. That damned Cator has already hit me up for his campaign. He wasn't too pleased when I told him the truth. I'd advise you not to lie to the district attorney. It's generally a bad idea." With that Jake hung up.

"Maye, we're causing some major heartburn in downtown Velda," Don said.

"I hope there's a fee in it." Maye had found time to get the names and addresses of the Evergreen protesters and their parents and sent off statements to each one For Services Rendered. "That should cover my salary for a few months," she said. "Those mothers and daddies don't want their little girls to have a record."

Baiting Jake and trying to protect Eugene from whatever scam his brother and Jake had cooked up was so much fun that Don almost forgot to be unhappy. But not quite. *The dreams still came. He should have been with Cecilia. He had no right to be alive and certainly no right to be happy.*

He tried to concentrate on the legal opinion from the Dallas law firm. He needed to understand it before Jake arrived. "I'm going for a walk," he said. He grabbed his coat and hat and went outside into a gloriously sunny, brisk Panhandle day. He circled the square, walked in front of the Phillips station and waved at Pete, who looked up from a flat tire that he was changing on a Chevy truck and waved back.

As usual, the antique shop on the northeast side of the square was closed. Josie only opened up on weekends and not always then. There wasn't too much drop-in traffic around the square, especially now that Elmer Thorpe's store had been converted

79

into a law office. Some of Elmer's regulars had tried to congregate there, reliving the old days, but Maye had shooed them away. "This is a place of business. Go smoke and drink and tell your stories somewhere else."

"Where else?" a rheumy-eyed retired pumper had asked plaintively.

"Go over to the VFW. Open that place up early."

And so they did. The VFW building was a run-down oil service equipment building that had been vacant since the oil boom before last, and in desperation, the owner had finally agreed to lease it to the VFW Post. Don resisted walking the block and a half to the Post. He didn't crave hearing inside jokes retold or anecdotes repeated. He just wanted to clear his head of the terrible memories that filled his dreams at night and crept up on him during the day, slamming him mercilessly without warning.

He was leaning against the Antelope statue when his phone rang. It was a text from Elmer. *"Don't need to sell water rights. Last Exxon well has come in big. Repeat big!!!"*

Don smiled. *One less thing to worry about.* He patted the Antelope on its flank and went back to the store and the damned legal opinion.

Jake was in no better mood when he drove his Cadillac to a screeching halt in front of the store. He nodded to Maye and looked around. "Nice furniture," he said. "Very familiar looking."

They sat across from each other in the conference room. Jake waited. Don brought out the trust document. "You really believe the Pervoy Trust gives the trustee the right to sell the water rights? All it says he can do is 'lease, sell or otherwise dispose of

80

the oil, gas and other minerals, including coal and sulphur.' Nothing about water."

"When it says 'other minerals' it includes 'water.'"

"Jake, you know better than that. There's a long line of cases that says 'other minerals' does not include 'water."

"They taught you that down at the old Confederate Law School? Did they forget to mention that in deciding what a trust means, the court looks at the intention of the grantor? Back in the 1930s George Pervoy never wanted the Pervoy Ranch sold. He wanted it for his heirs forever. So he created this trust. But he knew that the income would always come from the minerals. So he gave the trustee the power to lease or sell them. That's the only way the ranch could be kept together."

"You don't have to ask what the intent is when the trust is clear. This trust is clear. It doesn't include water."

"It does if all the beneficiaries agree that it does and the court confirms it. This just lets the beneficiaries get the income from the sale of the water rights. It's a once in a lifetime opportunity."

Don picked up the stipulation. "If Eugene signs this, and the attorney for all the kids and unborns doesn't contest, and the judge agrees, then the trustee can sell the water rights?"

Jake hesitated. "That's what it says. It's to all the kids' benefit."

"And the trustee is?"

Jake shifted in the wood chair a little uncomfortably. "It used to be Mary Marie Pervoy. When she resigned, Trey became the successor trustee. Strictly according to the Trust, which needs this money, Cuinn."

81

"The Trust or Trey Pervoy?"

Jake stood up. "That's insulting."

"You didn't say it wasn't true," Don said to his former employer's back.

When he was sure Jake had left, Don opened the file and took out the legal opinion from Filbert & Jacama, the opinion that he was pretty sure Jake did not know Faye had sent him.

CHAPTER ELEVEN

Maye laid the morning edition of the *Velda Sun* on Don's desk. "I hope you believe what they say, that bad publicity's better than no publicity."

"What's this?" Don looked at the blaring headline:

D.A. Says Local Lawyer Lied.

"This doesn't look good." He read the article, written by the editor of the *Velda Sun*:

District Attorney Richard Cator expressed surprise on learning that demonstrators at the Evergreen Plant had left the state without being charged under terrorism statues by federal authorities. Cator explained that local attorney Don Cuinn had agreed to deliver the protestors to federal authorities, but instead had released them and that they had apparently left the state.

"We're not even sure of their names," Cator complained. "It was a screw-up on our part, but we expected a member of the bar, an officer of the court, would do what he promised."

A caller to Rosen and Associates law office, where Cuinn is listed as an associate was told that Cuinn was no longer with the firm. He has apparently opened a law office in Antelope City, but could not be reached last night.

Federal authorities in Amarillo said the matter was under investigation."

Don went through the open door of Major Hansard's penthouse apartment. The large living room was full of people, and the smell of cigar smoke mixed with perfume. *Velda's A-List*, he thought.

A pretty redhead approached him. "Mr. Cuinn," she said, extending her hand. "I'm Bridget O'Neill. We talked on the phone. The major is happy you could come." The call had come the afternoon before, asking if he was free to attend the major's monthly open house the next evening.

Don wanted to say no, but he knew he needed to go, if only to see the result of being on the front page of the *Velda Sun*.

He shook her hand, "Hi. I've seen you around the building. Thanks for the invitation."

She led him to the bar. "Get a drink and something to eat. I'll tell the major you're here."

Don spoke to George and Tiny Poppoppolus, who were supervising the bar and laying out food on a long table at one end of the large room. "Is the Greeks shut down tonight?" he asked George, the older brother.

"Where are the chips?" George asked Tiny, who was round and bald, the opposite of his dark, tall slender brother. George turned back to Don. "Once a month we ask Mama to watch the store. It's a slow night. Most everybody is here." The two brothers' restaurant was the most popular in town. That is, it ranked first of two, the other being the Country Club. The Greeks' was the town's popular meeting place.

Don nursed a beer and surveyed the crowd from his spot at the bar. There were old men and young men in jeans and boots, a few men in suits, and lots of women, some young, some of a certain age. In one corner of the room, the major sat on a chair with double cushions.

He never stops trying to hide his shortness, Don observed.

From time to time, men approached Hansard, spoke softly and then retreated quickly. Bridget leaned over and whispered to the major. His eyes flickered up briefly. Bridget smiled at Don and motioned him over. Don returned the smile and made his way to the royal presence.

"Hello, Major. I'm Don Cuinn. We met at the Country Club."

They shook hands. Hansard's hand was icy cold, but hard as stone. "I remember. Was that the day you and Jake Rosen parted company?"

"You heard about that?"

Hansard motioned to Bridget and she slid a straight chair next to his. "Sit, please," Hansard said. "Yes, I heard." He handed his empty glass to the girl, who left them and strolled in the direction of the bar.

Despite himself, Don followed her with his eyes. He suspected that most of the other men in the room did the same.

He turned back to the major, who was smiling knowingly. "Bridget is my . . .assistant."

Don didn't answer. He didn't need to.

"It was probably time for you to leave Jake's practice, make a name for yourself."

Don laughed. "I seem to be doing that all right. If you saw the paper."

"*The Velda Sun*? Hardly influential in Velda, much less anywhere else in our world. Don't worry. Cator is covering his tracks for his race for district judge. Everyone understands that." He leaned close to Don and whispered. "He's over by the door, watching us, wondering if you might be under my protection, and that he might have offended me." Laughing broadly, Hansard patted Don on the back. "I'm glad we had this chat. I have some legal work I can send you. Work connected with water rights. I try to assist Velda's young lawyers to get established."

Don stood. *Water rights?* "That would be very good of you, Major. I need the business."

Hansard waved at Bridget, who returned with a full glass of Scotch. He took the glass. "Bridget, why don't you show Mr. Cuinn the view from the deck." He took a sip of the Scotch and said, "Don't stay too long. Bring him back and find Tommy Crackstone. They need to talk."

The girl took his arm and guided him to the deck, which was empty except for a couple sharing a joint. The sweetish smell blew across the deck.

Bridget was slender, with a boyish figure. She wore her red hair long. It contrasted dramatically with her paper white skin. She had on a dark skirt and a man's white dress shirt with the sleeves turned up. She wasn't a beauty queen but she was very attractive, in an alert, intelligent looking way.

He wanted to ask what her relationship was to the major, but he couldn't think of a way to ask without being very rude, as in, *Are you that little man's mistress?* He decided he really didn't care, so instead he said, "It's a great night, and a great sky, isn't it?" He had forgotten how to talk to a girl, even one he wasn't interested in.

"The evening sky is usually beautiful."

Don grunted. "Unless there's a tornado, or an ice storm, or maybe a dust storm. Or maybe all three at once."

Bridget looked up at him. "I'd say that you're a pessimist."

"Or a realist." He really didn't have a reason to be rude to this woman. Except for the picture of her with the major, which for some reason angered him.

They were silent for a few minutes, watching the sun set. The couple finished their joint and went back inside.

Bridget said, "I work for the major. I'm his secretary. Or as they say, his executive assistant."

"How long?" Don asked.

"All my life, it seems." She smiled.

She does have a very nice smile, Don told himself.

"Actually, it's been five years, ever since I got out of college." She nodded in the direction of the departing couple. "Would you like a smoke? I can find you some if you want."

He hadn't used since Cecilia's death, afraid to start down that path, as hopeless as he felt. "No thanks, not tonight. I'm in enough trouble with the D.A. He's right inside."

"Richard?" she said. "He's the biggest bong head of us all. It's easy to get. I can give you the name of a supplier, if you're interested. You may know him. Tipp Newton? The one who married the Pervoy girl?"

"Tipp? Yes. I know him."

They could hear the voices getting louder inside the penthouse. "If you think it's noisy now, wait 'til the real partying starts, after the major goes to bed," she said.

Don stood beside her and they watched the huge red sun fall quickly behind the horizon, leaving massive streaks of purple across the sky. "It is spectacular," Don admitted.

"I've always loved the sunset here."

"Have you lived here long?"

She inhaled deeply. "I was born here. I went to Catholic school, then to St. Mary's in San Antonio." My mother was a devout Catholic. My brother had to go to Notre Dame; I went to St. Mary's."

"She believed in education," Don offered.

Bridget settled on a wooden bench and he sat down beside her. "She believed in something better for us, even if she had to take in laundry, which she did until the major..."

Don waited for her to go on, not in any hurry for whatever was waiting for him inside. He was almost glad he had come.

"You probably wonder where my father was, during all that time?"

"It's none of my business."

"But it's heartless, isn't it, to leave his wife and family and go off in the middle of the night without even saying goodbye?"

"You should hear about my family."

"I'd like to." She paused for a long time. "The major and my mother were 'special friends' for several years. Even after that ended, he sent my brother Marcas and me to college, and gave me a job in his office. We owe him everything."

"I hadn't realized he was such a generous person."

"He has no family. He has Sunday dinner with us, after Mass. My brother or I look in on him at night, see if he needs anything, whether the housekeeper is behaving herself. He's lonely." She looked at her watch. "Oh dear, it's late. He will be ready to say good night."

They started back inside. "I still haven't heard about your family. How about dinner? Tomorrow night, maybe?"

Don shook his head. "I'm sorry. I wouldn't make very good company."

"Let me be the judge of that. Just call me."

He nodded and followed her inside. She waved at Tommy Crackstone who was standing by the door, talking to Hoppy Johnson, the landman.

She went across the crowded room and approached the major, who looked at his pocket watch, nodded brusquely, and walked stiffly through the crowd, which parted as he left. He nodded regally to the partiers, and shook Tommy Crackstone's hand at the door. Hansard waved to Donnie with a knowing look and left.

Strange little man, Don thought.

Don watched Bridget, who had joined George Poppoppolus at the food table. The dark Greek leaned down and whispered something in her ear. She laughed and patted him on the arm. They began straightening the table and putting out fresh glasses and liquor bottles.

Tommy Crackstone and Hoppy Johnson joined him. "Well, here we are. Apparently I'm supposed to offer you riches and fame if you'll allow Elmer Thorpe to sell us his water rights."

The room was already much nosier. Don leaned in closer to the Boston Brahmin. "Did I hear you right? You and Major Hansard are the local benefactors who are going to save Velda's water rights from Sawbucks Banjo?"

"It surprises you? I assumed you had worked that out."

"I did have my suspicions. Look, Elmer's not selling to Sawbucks Banjo. He doesn't want to sell to anyone. He doesn't need the money. He prefers to keep his water."

"Anyone can use three million dollars."

Don shook his head. "'That is a lot of money."

Hoppy broke in. "Five hundred an acre, for the Ogallala formation and deeper. You need to talk to him again."

"Before I do that, tell me why? It's hard for me to believe this is all for charity."

"What's in it for me, you mean?" Crackstone said. "You Irish. You cannot accept that sometimes people do things for the greater good."

"Bullshit."

"Talk to him," Crackstone said. "He is your client. No need for you to leave. I'm going." He motioned to Hoppy. "Let Mr. Johnson here introduce you around. There is a great deal of potential legal business in this room. People who respect what the major and I say. Even if you don't."

Reluctantly, Don followed Hoppy to a group of men, dressed in white dress shirts, ironed jeans, and boots. They had beers in their hands and were listening intently to a rather stocky man with longish black hair styled with what even Don recognized as a fifty-dollar haircut. It was Trey Pervoy. His bruises were almost all gone and his arm was no longer in a sling.

The group spread apart to let Hoppy and Don join them.

Hoppy introduced him to each one in turn, Bill Bradley, Jake Jackson, Jim somebody, Dave somebody, and then, clasping the stocky man on the shoulder, he said "And this is my favorite landowner, George Pervoy the Third. Trey, meet Don Cuinn."

"We've met," Trey said. He turned to the others. "This is the shyster who sneaked those demonstrators out of town."

The man named Jim spoke up. "Personally, I don't believe anything I read in the *Velda Sun*." He shook Don's hand. "Did you get some of that Boulder booty? As I recall from my days at OU, it was prime." The others laughed.

"I guess if I did, it would be in the paper, wouldn't it?" That drew another laugh.

Trey pulled Don aside and whispered. "You tell my brother to sign the damn papers, do you hear me?"

"And if I don't?"

"You don't want to go there."

Don looked around the room. "Where's your keeper, Trey? If Jake were here, he'd tell you not to threaten opposing counsel."

"He's not my keeper."

"We'll see you in court."

Elmer sounded suitably impressed when Don told him about the new offer for his water rights. "Lord help me, that's a lot of money."

"It is, Elmer. What I can't understand is why the major and Crackstone are doing this? What's really behind it?"

The line was silent for a minute. Elmer spoke first. "You'd think that Tommy Crackstone has everything in the world but he don't."

"How's that?"

"Well, his granddaddy started that company, over in the Ohio River Valley. Then his daddy came down here and built it into the world's biggest producer of whatever the hell it is they make."

"Acetic acid, I think."

"Like I said, whatever that is. Then it was Tommy's turn. The family sent him down to take over. And you know the first deal he made?"

91

"No, I don't believe I do."

"It was a big offshore drilling deal with Sawbucks Banjo. He ended up losing a chunk of the company's money. He's convinced Sawbucks cheated him."

"So he'd spend millions just to get even with Sawbucks Banjo? Would the family let him do that?"

"Who knows how those New Englanders' minds work? It's one theory, anyway."

"Interesting. But what about you and the three million? Are you interested or not?"

"I don't know, Counselor. It's found money, but if I take it, somebody I know will want to spend it. I'd rather wait and see how all this out here is going to work out."

"By 'all this' I suppose you're talking about your marriage. How is Lou Jo?"

"Oh, Lord, I am sick to death of this town. I'm thinking of coming home, buying a big house on the Gulch, living the rest of my days with friends and kinfolk."

"Is another re-divorce in the offing?"

"It would cost so much, or I'd already have you filing. Is there some state I could move where she doesn't get anything?"

"I doubt it, Elmer."

"Look into that, will you? Meantime, I don't want any more cash in hand. Tell those fellas I appreciate it, but I'll just hold on to the water rights for a while."

"Three million, Elmer. Even half of that is a lot of money."

"All of it's a lot more."

CHAPTER TWELVE

D on stood at the top of the west stairway entrance to the Velda County Courthouse, waiting for Eugene and Ginelle to arrive.

The courthouse had been restored to its 1920 beauty, thanks to a grant from the State Historical Commission's Courthouse Preservation Program. Proud of never taking federal or state aid of any sort, the Velda County Commissioners had watched with dismay as neighboring counties restored their courthouses with the newly available state funds. "None of them compares with our courthouse," County Judge Ike Ikers declared.

The Velda County courthouse was designed by Elmer George Withers in the Classical Revival style popular at the time. It was built of brick with columned porticos above monumental stairs. A cast stone balustrade framed a red clay mission tile roof above the two entrances.

Judge Ikers dragged two unhappy commissioners along to get a majority vote in favor, and Velda County applied for and got the grant. Ikers and the two complicit commissioners were turned out of office by enraged voters at the next election, but the work was already underway, and even the most vehement objectors confessed to liking the result.

Old partitions and false ceilings were removed; marble staircases were repaired; duplicates of original windows were installed. The main courtroom glistened with a restored plaster frieze. The tile floor with inlaid mosaic patterns, including a large star at the main corridor crossing, complemented the restored marble base, marble wainscot and plaster walls. The courtroom furniture was original, found languishing in attic storage. There was even talk of restoring the jail and sheriff's office, if Boom Gordon ever retired.

Don's clients arrived, dressed in their best finery. Eugene had on a stiffly starched white cotton shirt and a corduroy jacket. Ginelle had chosen her Sunday orchid-colored dress, with a little matching hat pinned to her hair. Inside the courtroom, Jake sat at the counsel's table on the right side. He was thumbing busily through some papers. Trey sat next to him, looking put-upon.

Wiley Franklin sat at the end of the table, not hiding how pleased he was with himself. *In court. In a real case. Even if only as guardian ad litem. He'll probably make as much as me out of this,* Don thought. He motioned for Eugene and Ginelle to sit behind the bar separating the tables from the spectators' area, and took a seat by himself at the empty counsel's table.

They sat silently, waiting for the judge to appear. He knew that Prudo Kelley and Jake were close.

Some months earlier, Jake had told him how he helped Kelley win his first election as district judge.

"I was an associate of Salado Jones. Salado was the biggest lawyer in Velda. Every oil company that did business up here had Salado on retainer. He was a giant of a guy, wonderful with the jury and a master legal tactician. One day he came in my office with a copy of a brief I had written in a case involving Texas water rights. I was just off the Harvard Law Review and I thought I knew how to write a brief. It was way too long,

94

two hundred pages. Salado tore off the cover and the front pages and said, "Come with me. We're going to pay a visit to Counselor Prudo Kelley.

"When we got to Kelley's offices, over in New Ophelia, he said, "Prudo, we have an important case. It involves groundwater rights and we need your help briefing the case.

"Kelley looked puzzled. He said, 'I'd love to help, but I don't know much about that subject.'" Salado laid my brief on the desk in front of Kelley and said, 'It's about $5,000 worth of briefing, I would say. This research may help you. Send me the brief when it's done. We'll add you as co-counsel. No need for you to come to court. Wouldn't want to interrupt your campaigning. Send me the bill and my client,' and here he named the largest oil company in the Panhandle, 'my client will gladly pay it.' Of course Prudo sent us back my brief, got his five thousand dollars from the oil company and was on his way."

Exactly at ten a.m., the bailiff, the clerk of the court, and the court reporter entered. The lawyers and the Pervoys struggled to their feet as the bailiff announced, "All Rise." Judge Prudo Kelley strode in, tugging at his black robe. He settled in behind the bench and opened a folder. He took out Jake's pleadings and looked at the three lawyers.

"Call the next case," he said to Milly Nelson, who had been Clerk of the District Court of Velda County, Texas for forty years.

Milly spoke with a strong Panhandle twang. "Cause No. 2012-200, 'In the Matter of the George W. Pervoy Family Trust dated March 1, 1932,' an Action for Declaratory Judgment."

Jake stood. "Jacob Rosen, appearing on behalf of the petitioners, Mary Marie Ardmore Pervoy, Belle Mada Pervoy Newton, and George W. Pervoy III, Individually, as Trustee of the Pervoy Family Trust and as guardian of his minor children George W. Pervoy IV and Mary Marie Pervoy Junior."

Jake nodded at Wiley, who stood, looked at the card in his hand and recited hesitantly, "Wiley Franklin, appearing pursuant to Your Honor's appointment as guardian and attorney ad litem of the unknown and unborn heirs of George W. Pervoy."

Judge Kelley nodded and looked at Don. "Do you represent a party here, Mr. Cuinn?"

"I do, Your Honor. I represent Eugene L. Pervoy, a respondent in this case and a beneficiary of the George W. Pervoy Family Trust, individually and as guardian of his minor children, Kansas City Pervoy, Dallas Texas Pervoy, and San Francisco Pervoy."

The Judge smiled. "Very colorful." The lawyers stood while the judge thumbed through the file. "This is an action for a declaratory judgment that the Pervoy Family Trust gives the trustee the power to dispose of the water rights. Is there any objection to such an order? "

Jake spoke first. "Not from my clients, Your Honor. They all agree that the trust should be so construed."

Jake looked at Wiley. "The unknowns and unborns also agree," the young lawyer said on cue.

The Judge smiled again at Don. "You're not going to make this easy, are you, Mr. Cuinn?"

"It is easy, Your Honor. The Trust is clear on its face. It does not grant the trustee the right to sell the water rights."

"So you object to the petition for declaratory judgment?"

"We do, Your Honor. My client," he said, turning to Eugene, "strongly believes that the water rights should remain in the control of the Pervoy trust in case they are needed in the future to maintain the Pervoy Ranch. Water and the use of the land are inseparably intertwined. He believes that George Pervoy never intended that the water rights be sold.

"Unlike oil and gas, which can be produced without endangering the use of the surface as a ranch, water is too precious and too essential. My client is prepared to forgo proceeds from selling the water to assure the survival of the ranch and he believes the trustee should do the same." In fact, Don was paraphrasing slightly what Eugene had told him. *Sell the water? Over my dead body, goddam it to hell!*

Don handed the clerk the filing that he and Maye had worked on for the last week. "I hereby move for a summary judgment, declaring that the Trust does not grant the power to the trustee to sell the water rights. In the alternative, we are filing a cross-action for a judgment that the trust is void on its face as a violation of the Rule Against Perpetuities, and a finding that all the trust assets, including the water rights, now belong to the three grandchildren of George W. Pervoy, share and share alike."

Jake stood back up, sputtering. "Your Honor..."

The Judge waived him off. "The Rule Against Perpetuities? Did you say the Rule Against Perpetuities?"

"Yes Your Honor. The Rule says that estates must vest within lives in being and..."

"I know what the Rule is, Mr. Cuinn. He looked down at Don's motion. "You have cases, I suppose. Ancient cases, no doubt."

"And modern ones too, Judge." He handed the clerk and the other lawyers a concise brief of the law, lifted in large part from the legal opinion from the Dallas firm of Filbert & Jacama that Faye had provided him.

"Your Honor," Jake said, "this is ridiculous. This will has been in force since the 1930s. It was drawn by Thomas Salado Jones, himself, the dean of the Panhandle bar. This is a stunt by Mr. Cuinn, who as we all know, isn't above such things."

"Even the Great Salado himself was guilty of error on occasion," the Judge said. "This will be my very first case, in all my years on the bench, involving the Rule. A fitting way to leave the bench, don't you think? If I do leave?"

Don smiled, enjoying Jake's discomfort. He could see Jake working it out, wondering if Faye had gone so far as to give Don the Filbert opinion. But Don had trapped him. Jake could not accuse Don of stealing the legal opinion without making public that the most prestigious firm in Dallas believed the trust was probably invalid. Even worse for Jake, Prudo Kelley had as much announced that there was no influence that Jake could bring on him. He must have learned that Jake was supporting his opponent. He owed Jake nothing.

Jake sputtered. "We need an opportunity to read this, this . . . this . . ."

"Brief?" Don offered.

"Of course, Mr. Rosen," the judge said. "Take all the time you need. God knows I'm in no hurry to rule. We could pass it on to the next term, maybe let my successor rule on it."

Trey tapped Jake on the shoulder and whispered in his ear. Jake said, "We want an early ruling, Your Honor. The question of the water rights needs to be resolved right away, for commercial reasons."

So Trey can sell them to one of the buyers before the offers go away, Don thought.

"Submit your briefs in a week, responses in a week after that. Oral arguments the first open day after that. Everyone agreeable?"

Jake and Don agreed. Wiley Franklin looked confused.

"Mr. Franklin," the Judge said, "the unborns may have more to lose here than anyone. You are their representative. I will want to hear from you in detail about the status of the Rule in Texas."

Wiley looked as though he had been hit in the head with the judge's gavel.

Not such an easy payday after all. Legal research probably isn't his strong suit, Don thought.

The hardest part was explaining the Rule Against Perpetuities to his clients. They sat with him in the back of the empty courtroom, trying to understand, but their eyes glazed over. "The Rule Against Perpetuities is an ancient legal principal designed to keep a person from forbidding his heirs from ever selling his estate. That would be a perpetuity, it would be a perpetual restriction, and the law doesn't favor perpetuities. For a lot of reasons, the law favors free transfers of inherited wealth."

Eugene yawned. He picked up his cowboy hat from the wooden bench and carefully stroked the crease. He wet his finger and rubbed a dusty spot.

Don went on, "The English courts came up with the Rule in the 1600s. It says that a person creating a will or a trust, like the trust here, can't tie up the property for longer than lives in being, plus twenty one years and nine months."

Eugene found a loose thread on his coat sleeve and pulled it free, winding it around his calloused forefinger.

"Here, your grandfather left the ranch to his son for life, then to his grandchildren, that is, Trey, Belle Mada and you for life, then to his great-grandchildren. On the face of it, that's too long. Great-grandchildren might be born later than twenty-one years after you three die, because George II and your mother might have had another child."

"That's crazy." Ginelle spoke up for the first time. *At least she had been listening* "They didn't have any more kids. They weren't even speaking by then."

"You're right. But the Rule doesn't work that way. It isn't what actually happened. It's what might happen when the trust was created, back in 1932."

Eugene got up, stretched, and yawned again. "It's just like I always told you, Honey. Lawyers don't care about facts. It's all make believe."

"I get it, Eugene," Don said, "but in this case the make believe may decide whether Trey can sell the water rights."

"I know I'm dumb," Eugene replied, "but tell me what happens if that Judge Kelley says the trust violated the whatchamacallit...?"

"The Rule? Just call it the Rule."

"Yeah. If he says the trust is bad on account of your Rule, then what happens?"

"Then the ranch would belong to you and Trey and Belle Mada, in equal thirds. Trey might be able to sell his share of the water, but I suspect anybody buying them will want 100%. It's just too complicated otherwise."

"That's no good. You know my sister. She'd sell out. The trust is a good thing. It keeps the ranch together, in the family."

"Let me argue it, Eugene. Jake and Trey aren't going to let it go that far. They'll give up on the water rights before they'll leave it to Judge Kelley to decide if the trust is valid or not."

Eugene looked at his plump wife. "He's the lawyer, Eugene," she said. "Let him do what he thinks is right."

CHAPTER THIRTEEN

"That landman is here," Maye called.

Don looked up and saw Hoppy Johnson at his door. He covered the trust lawsuit papers he was working on. "Have a seat, Hoppy. I was expecting to see you."

The skinny landman laid his stained Stetson on one oak chair and sat down on the other. "Nice day."

"Is it? I haven't been out."

"Busy in court, yanking Trey Pervoy's chain?" Don smiled.

"It's a strange business," Hoppy said.

"How so?"

"Well, there's Trey Pervoy, anxious as hell to sell his water rights, but he can't until he gets a clear title. Then there's Elmer Thorpe, who has a perfect title, who won't sell his for three million dollars."

"That is a paradox."

"Isn't it though? And who do we find, right in the middle of that paradox, stirring everything up, but prominent Antelope City lawyer Don Cuinn."

"I am prominent. I'm the only lawyer in Antelope City."

"Busy messing up my clients' playhouse."

Faye brought in coffee; then closed the door behind her. Don sipped the boiling hot coffee and waited for Hoppy to go on. The landman made a production of adding sugar and creamer to his coffee, stirring it, blowing on it, testing it, adding more sugar, testing it again, then setting the cup down on the desk. He stared at the cup. "Do you know why we call this the Antelope Play?"

103

"I didn't know you did."

"Oh yes. We have maps colored in yellow, tracts they want me and my employees to buy, buy limits, everything that makes up a land play. Except in this case, it's water, not oil and gas."

"And why do you call it the Antelope Play?"

"Because all of the tracts they want me to buy are centered on this town, right here, Antelope City." He spread his arms apart. "Right here in Antelope City, Texas. And you know what?"

"What?"

"The Pervoy Ranch and the Thorpe Ranch are flat dab in the middle of the play."

"The Antelope Play."

"Exactly." He took out a cigarette. "You mind?"

"I don't, but Maye does. She has adopted a no smoking policy since you were here last. I can't advise you to make Maye unhappy."

Hoppy shrugged and put the cigarette back in the pack. He shifted in the chair, then took an envelope out of his pocket and slid it across the table.

"What's that?" Don asked.

"I am instructed to offer you a retainer agreement for your legal services, for the next five years."

Don lifted the envelope by its corner. "That would make me the highest paid lawyer in Antelope City."

"Maybe in Velda, for all I know."

"And in return, I'm supposed to deliver Trey and Elmer?"

"There's nothing in there that says that."

"But even so, that would be the expectation."

"You would need to talk to them about that."

Don slid the envelope back to Hoppy's side of the table.

"Aren't you going to look inside, see what they're offering?"

"No. I might be tempted." Don leaned back in his chair. It squeaked. *Needs oiling*. "Tell me, is all this about Tommy Crackstone getting revenge on Sawbucks Banjo? If it is, you ought to know that Elmer says he will definitely not lease to Banjo. You can tell Tommy Crackstone that he's won."

"Maybe so. Our offer still stands. Mr. Crackstone and the major still want you on retainer." Hoppy picked up the envelope. "No deal?"

Don nodded.

"That's what I told them you'd say."

They rose and shook hands. "If it isn't about revenge, then what is it about?" Don asked.

"Damned if I know," Hoppy answered.

The Twin Beech Baron usually flew empty to the deserted private landing field outside of Laredo, but tonight there were two passengers. They got out of the black SUV and carefully stored a case of Bladnoch Scotch whiskey in the luggage section of the plane. "*Corresponde El Jefe*," one of them said to the other. "Es su favorito whisky. Bladnoch."

The plane took off into the midnight sky. George W. Pervoy III climbed to 20,000 feet and put the plane on auto pilot. Behind him, he could hear the two Mexicans talking and laughing in Spanish. He knew enough Spanish to tell they were talking about their girlfriends in the border town and whether they would have time to see them before picking up another load of cocaína.

Three hours later, Trey began his descent. He circled the Laredo ranch and the landing strip lights came on. He landed quickly and expertly, taxiing to a stop in front of the two black Cadillac SUVs, identical to the ones the *Venganza* cartel kept in Velda. He stayed in his seat while the men unloaded the whiskey and others brought the usual suitcases and strapped them down. Luis, the leader of the group, put his head inside the cockpit. He smelled of shaving lotion and cigar. "*El Jefe* says to tell you, only one hundred more trips and your debt will be paid." He laughed and clapped Trey on the shoulder. "Only one hundred!"

CHAPTER FOURTEEN

Don had given up on the Rule Against Perpetuities, at least for the night. He was sitting on his porch, nursing a beer and watching the sunset. A faded blue Corolla turned off the highway and drove up the west side of the square, past the newly repainted antelope statue and stopped in front of the office.

Bridget O'Neill got out of the car. She opened the passenger door and gathered up a large container covered with aluminum foil. From the porch, Don could smell the smoked brisket.

"You never called, so I thought I would invite myself to dinner," she said as she climbed the steps. "Where shall I put this?"

"It smells good," Don said.

"The Greeks never fail, you know that. Let's see, there's brisket and ribs and sausage, brown beans, coleslaw, pickles, apricots."

"I don't eat barbeque without Texas Toast."

"And of course Texas Toast." She looked around. "Where?"

Don rose and took the food from her. She brushed her red hair back and followed him to the kitchen. She watched while he tried to decide what to do with the food.

"Have you ever used your oven?" she asked.

"Not yet."

"Give it to me." She put the container in his oven, scrubbed sparkling clean by Maye or by someone she hired, and turned the dial to Warm. "There. It'll be ready whenever we are." She looked around. "Very nice. Any beer left?" She pointed at the empty Coors bottles on the table.

107

"Beer, wine, tequila."

"I'll have the beer, thanks."

After several beers, they demolished the food. Don had not realized he was hungry until he started eating. Contented, they moved back to the front porch.

"Get in the car," she ordered, "I want to show you something."

He locked the office and got in the passenger seat of the Corolla.

"Strap up."

He did as he was told, moved the seat back in an attempt to get more leg room, and asked, "Where are we going?"

"A place like you've never seen before." She gunned the little car and pulled out onto the empty highway, headed south. They were silent for the first ten miles.

'Tell me about your wife. I understand that she died."

"Yes."

"In an accident, I heard?"

"An accident. Yes, an accident."

"How terrible."

"My wife's name was Cecilia Rueda Medina. She was Mexican."

"How long were you married?"

"Not long enough." The memories flooded in:

A few short months, the happiest of his life. After a terrible misunderstanding, of course involving another woman and Donnie's stupidity, Cecilia had left Austin and returned to practice law in Mexico City. Donnie's last minute scholarship to work on Texas-Mexican relations at the University in Mexico City gave him a chance to try to make

108

*things right. But it had taken phone calls from his
mother and his stepfather, and even a kind word of
support from Cecilia's father, before she agreed to
see him. Once she saw the change in him, the
seriousness with which he was approaching his
work at the university, things progressed rapidly
and she took him back.*

*After a civil ceremony in Acapulco, they
were married in the chapel on her family's rancho,
in a valley on the side of Teotepec. His stepfather
and his mother flew to Acapulco for the wedding
and were ferried by limousine from the airport to
the hacienda.*

*His mother, Dorrie Louise, had never been
out of Texas before. She stood with Donnie and
Cecilia, admiring the view through the clouds to the
distant sea. "You will be very happy, with a
beginning like this," she had said.*

*And so they were. They spend their
honeymoon at Teotepec in the hacienda, alone
except for the servants, who had known Cecilia
since she was born and seemed to approve of her
choice of a husband. And of course, there were the
ever-present guards.*

"You must have loved her a lot."

"Yes, I did." Bridget's questions had snapped
him out of his reverie, but not for long:

*After a week at Teotepec, they returned to D.F.,
Distrito Federal, or Mexico City as the gringos
called it. Donnie moved from his room in the
student quarters in Coyoacán to Cecilia's
apartment across the Insurgentes in San Angel. It
was a honeymoon as long as they were together.
Many mornings she was late to work because he*

109

had to make love to her one last time, even after she was dressed and ready to leave. Many times he was home early from the library, too full of his thoughts of her to think about the Treaty of Guadalupe, picturing her in his arms.

Of course it could not last. Even he knew it was too intense to go on that way forever, but he knew that when the honeymoon was over, they would still be in love, with babies and good work to do and vacations at Teotepec as well as back in Texas. She showed him D.F., the parks and the shops, the cafes and the bars. She corrected his Spanish. A long happy life stretched before them.

It never occurred to him it would end as it did.

"You don't have to tell me about it if you don't want to," Bridget said, breaking the silence.

Why would I want to? The thoughts that haunted him would not, could not be voiced.

Donnie knew that Cecilia's father was a government official. He knew that he was high in the Ministry of Justice. He assumed that the bodyguards and escort cars were to protect the family from kidnappers. What he did not know, and what Cecilia never mentioned, was that her father was an important figure in the war against the Mexican drug lords. He was deeply involved in the Mexican Navy program that trained police officers to fight the cartels. They had been particularly successful against some of the supply routes of the Venganza Drug Cartel, which controlled much of the drug traffic in and out of the coast around Acapulco.

110

*It was Dia de los Muertos, the day when
Mexico honors its dead, and a two- day national
holiday. The family was to go to Acapulco by
private plane, and on to Teotepec by car, but
Donnie was delayed at the library.*

*"Just catch the next commercial flight,"
Cecilia told him. "One of the drivers will meet you
and bring you to Teotepec. If you want, I can wait
for you and we can come together."*

*Of course he told her, "No. There's no need
for that. I'll be along in a little while." He should
have asked her to wait.*

*The last words she ever said to him were
"Amo te, Donnie."*

*The driver named Paulo and a bodyguard
met him at the airport terminal. One took his
carry-on. They waited for him while he bought a
copy of Reforma. He was reading the sports page,
trying to find NFL scores when Paulo braked to a
sudden halt. They were rounding a tight curve in
the mountain road that led to Teotepec.*

Bridget blinked her headlights at a slow moving
truck and swung around it.

Ironic, Don thought.

*Local and federal police cars blocked the road.
Donnie recognized the black Mercedes and the
guard car. Both cars were turned on their sides.
"Jesus, no!" He jumped out of the still moving car
and ran toward the wreck. Two policemen held him
back. They were removing bodies from the
Mercedes.*

Bridget pulled off the highway onto a gravel road,
driving more slowly through the darkness.

111

Don sat up. "I need a drink."

"We'll be there in ten minutes."

"I said I need a goddamned drink!"

Holding the steering wheel carefully with one hand, she reached behind the seat and handed Don her carry-on. "There's a bottle in there."

Don fumbled with the bag. Stuffed between a nightgown and silk panties was an unopened bottle of tequila. He twisted off the seal and opened the top. He took a long drink of the familiar liquor, then a shorter one. He tightened the top and put the bottle back in her bag, trying not to touch her underwear.

The drink did not mask the memories. His mind continued to race:

Paulo explained to the policemen that Donnie was the espouso of the girl in the car and they let him through. By the time he got to the Mercedes, the bodies of Cecilia's father and her two brothers had been pulled from the car and were lying on the pavement. Their bodies were riddled with bullet holes and covered with blood. Her father's features had been blown away, but Donnie recognized his expensive gray silk suit.

He watched as two men pulled Cecilia from the car. Her face was unmarked, but she was covered in blood and she was dead. In one hand was the little Springfield XD handgun that her father had bought her when she left Mexico to study in Austin. Her father had been afraid of the violence in the States, Cecilia had told him. The dark beautiful girl wasn't killed instantly, despite what the papers would later say. She put up a fight.

He sobbed and she glanced over at him. "Do you want another drink?"

"No, I don't want another drink." *I should have been there. If I had been on time, there would have been another car with guards. I should have asked her to wait for me.* "It shouldn't have happened," he said at last.

"You can't blame yourself."

"You're wrong. I do blame myself. And I'm right."

They rode in silence until Bridget pulled the car up in front of a rock house. "Get out. I want to show you something. And bring my bag."

The moon was full and very bright. There were more stars than Don had ever seen in his life. He followed her onto the porch of the house. He held her bag while she unlocked the door. She tossed the bag into the dark house, then took his hand and guided him to the other side of the house. From there, he could tell the house was on the side of a steep cliff. The moonlight lit the rocks below them, and tall, jagged rocks cast shadows down the canyon face. It was a scene of fantasy, like a madman's painting of an alien landscape, colorless, but with countless variations of gray and black.

"Jesus. What is this place?" He leaned over the porch railing. He could not see the bottom.

"Careful," she said. "You've had a lot of tequila." She took his arm and put it around her shoulder. "You're on the north rim of the Palo Duro Canyon. It's about a mile down from here, and ten miles across."

"Whose house is this?"

"It belongs to the major. His father got it as a gift from the state for his help with the land purchase of the canyon. It was an old line house. It's been fixed up a little, but it's still pretty primitive. The major lets me use it. I love to come here and watch the sun rise and set over the canyon."

"It's amazing." Unaware, he had pulled her body close to his. He stepped away. "Bridget, thanks for bringing me here... and everything. But, I can't...I just can't."

"My poor broken boy." She stroked his face and pulled his head down and kissed him. "Come inside."

And somehow, he could.

When he did finally fall on her, he took her again and again, trying to drive away the nightmare and every thought except for the redheaded girl and her gift of her pale body in the moonlight that streamed through the windows.

He woke a little before sunrise. Bridget was sleeping soundly. He got out of bed quietly, pulled on his Jockey shorts and went out on the porch. The sun made its first appearance over the canyon rim, and the dark silhouettes of night were revealed to be columns of pink and blue and orange rock formations, sparkling and changing color with the approach of daylight. Bridget handed him a steaming cup of coffee.

"Thanks."

"My pleasure," she said, leaning against his bare chest. She was naked.

The memory of the night came rushing over him, but instead of arousing him, her body against his did the opposite. He felt a deep sense of guilt. He had betrayed Cecilia, and if that didn't make sense, he had surely betrayed her memory. He stood up. "I need to get back to the office. Can we go now?"

"It's still early," she said. She tried to put her arms around his neck, but he pulled away. "Oh," she

114

said, covering her breasts. "Let me get dressed and we'll leave."

When she pulled into Antelope City, he had not spoken the entire drive back from the canyon. He had shaken his head in refusal when she offered to stop for a breakfast taco at the Phillips station in Midway. Once in front of the office, she waited for him to say something.

He sat in the passenger seat, trying to decide what to say.

'When will I see you again?" she asked at last.

The office was dark. Maye hadn't opened up yet. "This wasn't a good idea, Bridget."

"I thought last night was good. I think you did too."

"You have no idea what I thought last night." He turned away and said, almost to himself, "Tell the major it didn't work." It was the most hateful thing he could think of to say.

"What did you say? Tell the major what didn't work?"

"He sent you out here to get Elmer Thorpe's water rights, didn't he?"

"Get out of my car, you bastard." She turned and hit him with both fists. "Get out!!"

He didn't watch but he could hear the little Toyota scream around the square and back on to the highway.

Why did I say that? He knew it wasn't true. *How did that make anything better?*

CHAPTER FIFTEEN

Don had run out of ideas how to apologize to Bridget. *Maybe it was better not to apologize at all. Maybe it was better to let the bitterness be,* he reasoned. At least he wouldn't be tempted to be unfaithful to Cecilia's memory again. *You're crazy. Cecilia wouldn't want you to be like this.*

He was almost desperate enough to ask Maye for advice, but she would probably tell him to kill his miserable self and be done with it. The phone rang. He answered. At first, he could not place the familiar voice.

"Is this Don R. Swinn?" The caller spoke with the hard nasal Panhandle twang.

"It's Cuinn."

"It's spelled "Swinn," the man said argumentatively.

It was the self-assured belligerence that identified the man as Sawbucks Banjo, the scourge of the airways and financier *par excellence.* "Actually," Don said, "that's the original Irish spelling, 'C.u.i.n.n' not 'Q.u.i.n.n', but you can pronounce my name any way you want to, Mr. Banjo."

Banjo accepted as his due that he had been recognized. "Whatever," he said. "I've heard you control a big piece of water rights in Velda County."

Don could hear a prompting voice and the roar of a jet engine. *A private jet,* Don assumed.

"A rancher named Thorpe? I'd like for you to come over to Amarillo so we can meet each other and discuss it. Say tomorrow morning. I'm flying out at one o'clock."

117

"Well sir, Mr. Thorpe controls his own water rights. I'm just his lawyer."

"I'm told by my land manager here that Thorpe referred anything about the water to you," Banjo pressed. "So can you be there by ten or not?"

"I suppose I can," Don began.

"See you then." Sawbucks Banjo hung up abruptly.

Don did not know the address of the offices of Amarillo's biggest celebrity, but he suspected Maye knew the place.

Maye gave him the address. "Sawbucks. What a name. So you're going to meet the big man himself? You're really coming up in the world."

"Actually, I've already met him...in Austin...through a friend of mine who used to work for him."

Maye look unimpressed.

"Wesley Bird. He played football at U.T."

Now Maye was impressed. "Wesley Bird? You are a friend of Wesley Bird? The All-American?"

"Used to be a friend is more like it."

"Oh Lord, I may faint," Maye said. She went so far as to sit down in Don's chair.

"Are you all right?"

Maye picked up Don's *Rule Against Perpetuities* brief and fanned herself with it. "Wesley Bird. Oh my, I loved to watch that boy play football. He was like a Greek god. Do you remember the pass he caught, the winning touchdown in his last Texas-Oklahoma game?"

"Who could forget?" He had, for one. "So you're a University of Texas fan?"

"One of the few in the Panhandle. Now Faye, she's an Oklahoma fan. We have seats right on the fifty- yard line in the Cotton Bowl. I wear my Burnt

118

Orange pant suit that I ordered from Sue Patrick's down in Austin, and she wears some crappy red thing and we sit right next to each other."

"Right at the dividing line."

"Yes. Right there. Oh, what a time we have, yelling at each other. I sing *The Eyes of Texas* and she sings *Boomer Sooner*. The loser has to drive home and the winner gets to gloat and drink whiskey sours. For six hours. Even Faye drinks if OU wins." She fanned herself some more. The *Rule Against Perpetuities* brief fell apart and scattered on the floor. Maye was too excited to notice. "So tell me. Is Wesley Bird as good looking up close as he was on the football field?"

"The co-eds thought so."

Maye giggled. "I'm not surprised. I read that he married that Patson girl, daughter of one of the richest men in Texas?"

"Yes. He did."

"What a lucky girl."

"Lucky."

Don didn't tell Maye her hero was a fraud and a jerk and that he was probably miserable being a kept man in the Patson family. At least Don hoped he was miserable. He had never cared much about Sawbucks Banjo, one way or the other, but he had fired Wesley Bird when Wesley tried to solicit Banjo's investors to finance Wesley's aborted race for Congress. At least Don would approach tomorrow's meeting believing that was in Banjo's favor.

"Let's hear what he has to say," he told Elmer when they talked on the phone.

A famous energy expert and manager of large funds who invested in energy projects, Banjo was a well-known television personality. Recently, he had

119

seized on water shortages in downstate Texas as a new source of riches. His paid experts forecast huge increases in the demand for water in Dallas and Fort Worth for those cities' growing populations and expanding industries. The problem was that the rivers and lakes and underwater reservoirs nearby were not adequate to supply their future needs.

The scantily settled Texas Panhandle, on the other hand, sat atop vast water supplies, and Banjo visualized a three hundred mile pipeline running south to Dallas and Fort Worth, delivering the water they needed so badly. All it took was money, government permits and approvals, and the rights to the underground water, much of which was owned by ranchers around the Velda area.

As far as Don could tell, Sawbucks Banjo was contracting to lease the water rights from the ranchers, agreeing to pay big prices, but all on option agreements. The ranchers would get paid if the deal came together, and it appeared from the newspaper reports that the options had only a few months to run.

Banjo was deep in negotiations with a group of Texas cities to sell them his positions in Velda water rights and cash out his investment. He would realize a big payday for having the idea and assembling the block of water rights.

Don sat in the reception area of S.B. Inc., Sawbucks Banjo's company, reading a sports magazine. He was early for his appointment, because he had allowed time to find the office. As Maye had told him, it occupied the entire top floor of the tallest building in downtown Amarillo, so it was not hard to find. Downtown was nearly deserted, with boarded-up storefronts and vacant streets. Business

120

had apparently moved somewhere else. The office was eerily quiet; no one came or went from any door of the top floor.

Don remembered reading about a feud Banjo fought with the local tax assessor. When he didn't get his way, he moved his hundred employees and all his operations to Fort Worth, where he was welcomed with open arms. "Wait 'til they get to know him," the local official was quoted as saying. All that was left of S.B. Inc. in Amarillo was this office, and so far as Don could tell, the only occupant was a very blonde receptionist. "Good morning?" she asked with an English accent.

Don introduced himself. She turned aside Don's opening line, "How does an English girl end up in Amarillo?" with a polite if frosty smile.

"Mr. Banjo will be here soon. He's flying in from Chicago this morning and his plane is already on the ground," she said.

Only thirty minutes late, Sawbucks Banjo burst through the door, followed by a tall, overweight man carrying two overstuffed briefcases. Banjo ignored Don. He took a handful of messages from his secretary and hurried into his office. He yelled at the girl, "Diet Coke, Shelley."

The overweight man put down the briefcases and said, "You must be Elmer Thorpe's lawyer?"

"Don Cuinn." They shook hands.

"I'm Chisholm Petticure. Thanks for coming. We're running a little late." He grinned. "We're always running a little late." He called to Shelley, who was rushing into Banjo's office with a glass of ice and a Diet Coke. "I could use one of those too, Shelley."

The English girl ignored him and returned to Banjo's office. Don could hear her running through his appointments.

Petticure handed Don his card. "He'll be ready to talk to you in a minute. Would you like a Coke, or coffee?"

"It doesn't look like a good time for that. I'm fine, no problem." He looked at the card. It gave Petticure's Fort Worth address and his title "Vice President, Land."

Vice President and Briefcase Carrier, Don thought.

When Shelley finally told them to go into his office, they found Banjo seated behind a ten-foot desk. Computer screens and flat television sets lined one wall. Two exterior walls were glass and through them Don could see the rest of Amarillo to the west and beyond that, miles and miles of flat rangeland. Don took a seat across the desk, waiting for Banjo to speak. Finally, the busy entrepreneur looked at Don and said, "Well, what can I do for you?"

Petticure spoke up, "This is Don Cuinn, Sawbucks. He represents the Thorpes, their water rights."

"Oh. Right." Sawbucks Banjo looked tired, his bad skin was puffy around his face. He was thin but his jowls sagged. He rubbed his eyes. "So what does he want for his water?"

"He doesn't want to lease, Mr. Banjo."

"Doesn't want to lease, or doesn't want to lease to me?"

Don hesitated, trying to decide how much to tell Banjo and Petticure, who was busy taking notes. "He's turned down another offer, for more than you offered."

"How much more?"

122

"Considerable. Cash."

"He turned down a higher cash offer? That would have been from Tommy Crackstone, right?"

"I'm sure you're familiar with everything that goes on in Velda."

Banjo leaned back in his leather chair and stared at Don through sleepy eyes. "Do you know much about water?"

Don smiled. "Just to drink. And that everybody needs water to live."

"Exactly!" Banjo said, jumping to his feet. "You have to have water to live, and there are millions of people who live where water is absent. That's the basic dilemma. Now if you could get all those people to move out here, to the beautiful Panhandle," he said, gesturing out the window at the miles of empty spaces, "why, there'd be no problem." He paused for effect. It was obvious he had given the speech many times before. "But for some reason they don't want to do that. They want to stay in Fort Worth and Dallas. Even Austin, God forbid."

"You dislike Austin?" Don asked.

"Pinko, left-wing sewer of the universe, my personal opinion. But that's neither here or there. Even tattooed, wild-haired liberal slackers need water. But the water's not down there. At least not enough for ten or twenty years down the road. It's here, right here, in the best tasting, best flowing, easiest to produce, largest underground reservoir in the State of Texas! The Ogallala aquifer! Right here!" He paused, staring at the ceiling as if waiting for divine inspiration before continuing. "So what's the answer?" he asked quietly, staring at Don. "What's the answer? Move the people or move the water?"

Don played his part. "Move the water, I guess."

"Exactly!" Banjo shouted again. "Move the goddamn water! Move the goddamn water! It will happen, or my name isn't Sawbucks Banjo."

It isn't, not really, Don thought.

Banjo sank back in his leather chair again, gathering strength for Part Two of his sermon.

"Look here," he said. He took a remote control from his desk and turned on the sixty-inch monitor hanging on the wall. A map of the Texas Panhandle appeared. "Here, in these five counties," he said, pointing at a large area colored yellow, "there's 125 million acre-feet of Ogallala water." He paused for effect. "Do you know how much water that is?"

"A lot?" Don guessed.

"Damn right it's a lot. There's 326,000 gallons of water in an acre foot. I'm guessing you're not a math major, but that comes to about 41 trillion gallons of water. Think about that, 41 trillion!"

He went on. "The average Texan uses about 65,000 gallons of water a year. That's less than one fifth on an acre foot. In other words, if we can move, I mean, *when* we move, 400,000 acre-feet of water a year to the south, we'll be taking care of the annual needs of nearly two million Texans. And we can do that for over 150 years and still have lots of water left for irrigation and any needs of the towns up here. Plus the Ogallala recharges. It'll never run out."

He went back to the desk, staring intently at the screen. Don finally ventured a question. "How much will all this cost? Will people be able to afford the water when it gets to them?"

"They can't afford not to have it," Banjo said. "It'll be competitive with any other water supply. But you're right, it is an expensive project. Acquiring the water rights is important, but the most expensive part is laying a pipeline to take the water south. That's a billion dollar project."

Don waited.

"A billion dollars. Sure, I could do it. I can raise that much, but I've got other things to do. That's why I've made a deal to sell my water rights to the cities. Let them do the pipeline. When people start to be squeezed, the cities will have to do it and their rate payers will be happy to pay for it."

Meanwhile, you're making a fat profit flipping the water rights.

"Let's get back to Mr. Thorpe. We need the water rights under about 300,000 acres of land to support our project. I've already got a lot of that under contract. The missing pieces are Thorpe's and the Pervoy Ranch. The cities have to have the whole 300,000 acres, or the deal may collapse. So I'll ask you again. How much does Thorpe want?"

Don looked at Petticure and shrugged. *Tell the man I'm serious.* "Mr. Thorpe doesn't want to sell. And if he changed his mind, I think he'd favor the Antelope Water Conservancy, because that's cash up front."

"The Antelope Water Conservancy? Is that what Crackstone and Hansard call it?"

Don nodded.

"At first I thought this was all about Tommy Crackstone hating me for...you know that history?"

"I've heard rumors."

"Let me tell you about that. I had a high-risk, high-return offshore drilling project. Tommy was new in town. The Crackstones sent him down here

125

to learn the business. He was green as hell. He came to me, looking for some higher returns than the chemical business. I guess he wanted to impress the folks back east. I told him it was very high-risk before he signed on, but he got his daddy to approve it and said that he wanted in."

Banjo drank the last of his Diet Coke. "Unfortunately, the well was dry and we lost a bundle. Naturally, he blamed me. He told his old man that I cheated him. It was better than admitting he'd tried to play with the big boys and lost. The next well was a major discovery, by the way, but by then, Crackstone was out of the picture."

"You think Tommy Crackstone's spending millions on water rights to get even with you because of that?"

"At first I did. But now, I think there's something else. I don't know, it just doesn't feel right." Banjo pulled out a map of Velda County and spread it out on the desk. "Does anything look funny to you?"

"What do you mean?"

"Everything in yellow is what I've got tied up. And here," he said, pointed at several uncolored tracts, "are the Pervoy Ranch and Thorpe's land and some smaller parcels. And this," he said, spreading a beefy hand over a large tract colored red, is the Evergreen Plant. If Crackstone signs Pervoy and Thorpe, and gets those others, they'll have every ranch that abuts the Evergreen Plant, for a distance of several miles to the east."

"So?" Don said. "Can you think of a reason they are buying up the water rights next to Evergreen?"

Banjo stared at him. "No. I cannot"

Liar.

126

Banjo paused and then said, "Look, I'm in a hurry. I'm on the air in five minutes with that good-looking girl who hosts the Wall Street Hour. If you find out what Tommy and the major are up to, give me a call." He brushed past Don.

Don and Petticure stood in front of the screen in the reception room and listened to Sawbucks Banjo predicting $200 a barrel oil prices.

"There's no doubt," he asserted.

Don made a note to check how much S.B. Inc. stock went up after today's performance.

CHAPTER SIXTEEN

"Google everything you can about the Evergreen Plant," Don said to Maye over his cell phone.

"No cell phones while driving," she admonished him.

He called her back. "Especially anything about water."

"You're not hands free are you?"

He called her back again. "Especially about the Ogallala formation."

"Is that it?" she asked. "It's useless trying to talk sense to you. Remind me to get you a Bluetooth."

Don ignored her. "There's some reason the Antelope Group wants the land abutting the plant site. Maybe the government needs the water. That could be it. They're planning to sell at a premium to the government. There has to be a scam in this deal somewhere." He was trying to make sense of it all when Jake Rosen called.

"Listen, Don. You and I need to talk. There are some things I need to explain to you before the hearing."

"Are you getting worried that Judge Kelley might follow the law?"

"Well, I am worried that he might shaft my clients because I'm supporting Cator."

"He didn't seem real happy."

"We need to get this resolved before the hearing. Meet me at the Greeks. I'll buy you lunch and we'll see if we can't work it out."

"I certainly won't turn down a free lunch from Jake Rosen."

The Greeks was a combination restaurant, deli, coffee house, bar and pool hall. The two brothers, George and Tiny Poppoppolus served the best steaks in town. At the luncheonette counter, Velda regulars lined up for the fat hot dogs covered with onions and the Greeks' red-hot chili. A pair of dark curtains shielded the dining room. In a room off one side of the dining room were a bar and pool table. On the other side were three small private rooms. Tiny, three hundred pounds and sweating heavily, looked up from the grill on which a dozen franks were simmering and pointed to the back.

Don went through the curtains. The dining room was empty, but he could see Jake in the middle private room talking to George Poppoppolus. Unlike his brother, George was trim, well groomed and collected. He spoke to Don and then left them alone. He closed the door behind him.

"I got us a couple of rib eyes and a pitcher of beer, if that's all right with you," Jake said.

"Fine." Don sat across from his former employer.

They chatted about the weather, the first topic of conversation any day in Velda. This was another fine day, but we might still get a late season storm. Wouldn't some rain be nice? Do you see that tornado down in Guthrie? The second topic was the Dallas Cowboys. How they lost their last game in overtime; how their owner was an idiot. "But a very wealthy idiot," Don interjected.

The beer came. Jake filled both frosted mugs, took a long sip and got down to business. "The *trust* needs to sell those water rights. The *trust* needs the income."

Don took a drink of beer and wiped his mouth with the oversize white linen napkin. "Really? With oil prices like they are?"

"The ranch has a lot of gas wells on it. Gas prices are down." He looked at Don, who didn't reply. Jake went on. "Expenses are up. The money for distributions to the Pervoys is way down."

"Does Eugene need to ask for an audit?"

Jake shook his head. "No, no, that's not a good idea."

"Why not?"

"The Pervoys don't want to air their dirty laundry in public. This is a Pervoy family deal. We need to keep it that way."

There was a tap on the door.

"Come on in," Jake said."

George and a busboy brought in their steaks, a plate of home fries, and iceberg lettuce salads covered with the Greeks' famous house dressing. The steaks were sizzling in their juices on stainless steel platters. "Anything else?" George asked.

"Maybe another pitcher," Jake said. "And thank you, George. The steaks look great."

The thin Greek nodded to his helper who scurried out and brought back another pitcher of beer.

The two men turned to their steaks. They ate silently for a few minutes, washing down the rare grilled beef with swallows of cold beer. Don cut a piece of the steak and examined it on his fork. "You mentioned dirty laundry?"

"Just an expression."

"But Trey, as Trustee, wouldn't want the trust's books to be audited, is that right?"

Jake looked nervously around the little room. He pushed the door fully closed with his lizard boot.

"All right. This is strictly between us. Settlement talks; all that shit. Completely confidential and... un...and I do mean *un*repeatable. O.K.?"

Don nodded.

"Trey is in a bind. He put a lot of money in a Laredo bank and it didn't pan out."

"Laredo? Even I know Laredo's not the center of the banking business."

"As he explains it to me, the trust needed the high returns."

"Why?"

Jake pushed his empty plate aside. "To replace the money he lost."

"Come on, Jake. Don't make me drag this out of you."

"Unrepeatable, right?"

"Yes. Just tell me."

"Trey has a couple of problems. He has a drug habit problem and he has a gambling problem."

"Jesus. Are you telling me that Trey used trust money to buy drugs and to gamble?"

"So you can see why we need to work this out in private. He could go to jail. He's already lost his wife. Margaret's taken the kids and gone home to Oklahoma. This would about kill Trey's mother, if she found out. He's all alone out there. His only hope is to sell the water rights and replace the money he lost."

"Jesus."

"If you break the trust, it'll be even worse. Then everybody will know that the money's gone."

"You know I have to tell Eugene about this, don't you?"

"Goddamn it, Cuinn. You just promised."

"It's Eugene's decision, isn't it?"

"He'll do whatever you tell him. You don't have to tell him everything."

"You know I do, Jake."

Jake looked even wearier than usual. "Shit. I wish I'd never heard of the Pervoys and their damn problems."

Don was sitting on the edge of his bed, pulling on his boots and trying to decide what to advise Eugene at their meeting at the Pervoy Ranch that afternoon when there was a knock on the bedroom door.

"Mr. Cuinn," Maye said. "Are you decent?"

"Come on in, Maye." He looked up at the unflappable woman standing in the doorway. She looked flapped. "What is it?"

"There's a man here to see you. From Washington?" She handed him the card. It read "Bustin Johns, Investigator, Anti-Terrorism Task Force."

Don handed the card back to her. "Too late to escape out the back, I guess. They probably have a SWAT team out there anyway."

Maye attempted a smile, but failed. "What shall I tell him?"

Don pulled his right boot on. He stood up. "Tell him I'll be right with him. But bring me a cup of coffee, please. I need it."

Maye had put Johns in the conference room. He was looking at Don's diploma.

"What can I do for you?" Don asked.

Johns turned and smiled at Don. "No, sir. It's what I can do for you."

"I like that better. Have a seat."

"I'll get right to the point, Mr. Cuinn."

Don shrugged. "I'm all ears."

"Mr. Cuinn, you have become a person of interest to the ATTF. I'm here to investigate and produce a recommendation about what, if any action the task force should take in your matter."

"I'm a 'person of interest' in a terrorism investigation? Really?" He thought a minute and then called out. "Maye. Come in here please."

Johns raised his eyebrows.

"I've learned in my long legal career that it's always best to have a witness present in affairs involving a private citizen and his government."

"You learned that in Austin?"

Of course Johns knew about Don's run-in with then Texas Attorney General Eben Payne V. "There and here. I suppose you're here because of my conversation with our district attorney."

Johns opened his briefcase and took out a file. He flipped through it. "According to Mr. Cator, he released terrorist suspects into your custody on your promise to turn them over to law officers in Amarillo."

"I never promised Mr. Cator anything. And, they weren't terrorists. They were innocent protestors."

"How can we be sure of that? We were never able to question them. We don't even know their names."

"They were a bunch of college students. They're back in school now."

"Of course you will furnish us their names?"

Don winked at Maye. *Never fear.* "I'm afraid I can't do that. Those are my clients."

"Hindering a criminal investigation is a serious matter, Mr. Cuinn."

"I'm a member of the Bar."

Johns looked up at Don's diploma. "Ah yes. Where is the Jefferson Davis School of Law?"

"I have a feeling you know the answer to that." He stood up. "Are we done?"

"No, no. Sit down, please. As I said, I'm here to investigate and recommend. It seems to me that you may be the victim of an unfortunate misunderstanding."

Don looked at Johns with suspicion. *Where the hell is this going?*

"If what you say is true, that the protesters were college kids involved in a harmless demonstration, then maybe we can resolve this matter and the task force can move on to more important things."

"It is true."

"It's just your word, isn't it?"

"You can ask any of your task force. They were at the Evergreen Plant gate when it happened. They know those girls aren't terrorists."

Johns turned some more pages in the file. "Maybe they would say that. Maybe they wouldn't. No, I was thinking of something else."

"Like what?"

He shoved two pieces of paper across the table. "These are affirmations of your good character. Get them signed by two prominent citizens of Velda and this matter will be closed."

Don looked down at the documents. "Two prominent citizens? Like who, for instance?"

"I've made some inquiries. From what I'm told, if Major Cavendish Hansard and Mr. Thomas Crackstone were to vouch for you, that should be more than adequate."

"And if they don't?"

135

Johns stood. "Well, in that case, I would have to report the facts and your case could be referred to a grand jury for possible criminal prosecution under the anti-terrorism statutes. Those cases can be very messy, last a long time. And have very severe penalties."

"I see." *He didn't, though. It did not make sense.*

Johns gathered up his papers. He laughed. "Let's not make a federal case out of this. You have my card. Get the affirmations to me in Washington and all will be well"

CHAPTER SEVENTEEN

Eugene was waiting for him at the Pervoy Ranch gate. On the drive to the ranch, Don had tried to digest the concept of an ATTF investigator calling on him in Antelope City, but just thinking about it gave him a headache. *It's no use. Concentrate on Eugene and his problem. That's all you can do.* He parked outside the gate, climbed over and joined Eugene in his new truck. *A new one?* Somehow, Trey had found the money to buy Eugene a new truck.

On the drive up to the old ranch house he explained to Eugene that his brother had looted the Pervoy Family Trust and that selling the water rights might be the only way out. Eugene stopped, got out and kicked the tire as hard as he could.

"Don't dent it. It might be awhile before you get another one."

Back inside, Eugene started the truck with a roar. "Shit. I didn't need a new truck. Trey sent Elmer Maclain out with it, after you didn't get me out of jail." Elmer was the Ford dealer. "I should have been suspicious, Trey acting so nice, even to Ginelle." He pulled to a stop in front of the old house. Ginelle was standing in the doorway, her figure casting an outsized shadow. "Trey always was a fool. But stealing from the family. Jesus Christ. I never would have thought."

They sat around the oak table in the kitchen. Ginelle poured big glasses of sweetened ice tea and then settled into the kitchen chair across from Don.

"Well?" she said. "What is it?"

Don repeated his explanation.

When he was finished, she leaned over and patted Eugene on the cheek. "I'm so sorry, hon. I always knew he was no good. Just born that way. No good."

Eugene drew back and slapped her hand away. "Don't you talk about my brother that way, you hear? Trey and me promised my Daddy on his deathbed we'd look after each other. It don't matter what Trey has done, I mean to keep my promise. In this house, with our kids, he's still family, and I won't hear a word against him. Have you got that, Ginelle?"

Tears welled up in her blue eyes and rolled down the creases of her plump cheeks. "I'm sorry, honey."

"Now that's settled," Eugene said, looking at Don, "how do we go about straightening this mess out?"

Don parked in his old spot outside the HanRo Building. He had called Jake on the way back to town. Jake was waiting for him when he got off the elevator.

Faye fussed over him like he was the prodigal son returning. "Just leave him be, Faye. He doesn't need any more coffee. He doesn't want a Diet Dr. Pepper."

"Now just a darned minute, Jake," Don said with a grin. "I'd love a Diet Dr. Pepper, Faye, thank you."

"With ice, Mr. Cuinn."

"Oh for God's sake. Just close the door, Faye. We need to talk. You can pet him later."

When they were alone, Don said, "This is a bad deal all around, isn't it, Jake? Eugene is really shook up."

"It is. Yes. It's so bad that Margaret has left and taken the children back to Oklahoma."

138

"Yes, you told me." *It almost made him feel sorry for Trey.*

"Old man Aspen doesn't want Trey anywhere near the Aspen money. The pre-nups run both ways in that marriage. Margaret called her Daddy when Trey asked her for money. I expect a divorce petition any day now."

"Jesus. How is Mary Marie taking it?"

"Well. She's his mother and he's her darlin'. I'm sure Trey has borrowed from her. I can't imagine she knows how bad things are. It'll about kill her if she finds out." Jake stood and looked out the window. Velda sparkled in the bright sunlight. "We sure could use some rain," he said. "So tell me some good news, Donnie Boy. I could really use some good news."

"I'm the bearer of glad tidings," Don said.

"Yes?"

"Eugene will agree that the water rights can be sold by the trustee. But, on advice of his counsel, he cannot agree that Trey should continue as trustee. There should be a new trustee, who will make sure the money from the sale goes where it's supposed to go, replacing the money that Trey...ah...mis-appropriated."

"As far as that goes . . .?"

"All prior acts of Trey as trustee will be ratified and he'll be discharged without recourse."

"That's generous of Eugene."

"I thought so too. It's what he wants. He's thinking of the Pervoy family first of all. It's a pity his brother didn't do the same."

"Yes." He nodded his head. "And for the new trustee? Maybe the bank here, or in Amarillo? Or even Dallas?"

"No."

"No? Then who?"

"We talked about it. It seems to me that the only way to keep this in the family is for Eugene to be trustee."

"Eugene? Are you joking?"

"That's our proposal. Eugene as trustee or no deal."

"That's going to be hard for Trey to accept."

"Harder than the federal pen?"

A dozen cut, long-stemmed bright red roses graced a vase on Faye's desk. "Could I have one of those?" Don asked. "I have an apology I need to make."

She wrapped it in a piece of paper and handed it to him. "I saw her come in a while ago. Good luck."

"Thank you. I believe I will need it."

Bridget looked up from her computer screen when he opened the door to Major Hansard's offices. Everything was furnished in Depression era, 1930's style, oak. An old upright Underwood typewriter stood on a table in the corner, awaiting the ghost of secretaries past. "The major's not here," she said.

"Good." Don handed her the rose. "This is for you. I'm really sorry."

She hesitated, then took the flower and laid it on her desk.

"I promised myself never speak to you again."

"I guess you decided to, anyway." He smiled.

"I guess I did."

"I hope we can be friends." *He remembered her naked body that night at the Canyon.*

"I hope so too."

He waited awkwardly, trying to decide what to say next. *He wanted to see her again, but his*

140

memory of Cecilia was too strong. Would it always be this way?

"I owe you an apology, too," she said at last.

"Me? Why?"

"When I got back here," she said, "the major asked me if I thought you had changed your mind about selling the water rights." She held the rose close to her face and sniffed it. "I told him I had no idea." She put the rose down. "So pretty. I have a vase here somewhere." She smiled faintly. "Then he said, did I think I might persuade you?"

"What did you say?"

"I told him I doubted it very much."

"Well," Don said. "You're pretty damned persuasive."

"Am I? I wouldn't have thought so. But anyway, you were justified in being suspicious. So I'm sorry."

"Friends?" Don asked.

"Friends," she answered.

CHAPTER EIGHTEEN

Faye met him as he left the major's offices. "Boom says he needs to talk to you. He says he'll meet you in the deputies' parking lot."

"Did he say what about?"

"No sir, he did not."

Don drove to the deputies' lot and spotted Boom leaning against an empty patrol car, his Stetson pulled low over his eyes against the bright sun. He waved Don over and tapped on the window on the driver's side of Don's truck. Don rolled down the window.

"What's up, Boom?"

"I have this message for you. You are to call this number." He handed Don a slip of paper. "Be careful what phone you use." He turned and walked away.

Don did not recognize the number. He folded the paper and put it in his shirt pocket. Instead of going directly back to the office, he drove out the loop to the Wal-Mart, where he bought a cell phone and a prepaid wireless card. He walked away from his truck to one side of the building and looked around to be sure he was alone. *I'm paranoid. That doesn't mean people aren't listening.*

He recognized the voice on the other end of the line. "Hello, Lawyer."

"Hello, Maggie," he answered. "Did you lose my card?"

"Oh, it's right where I put it, reminding me of you."

"That's nice." He smiled to himself, remembering the pretty college student slipping his

143

card down the front of her sweater. "So, why all the cloak and dagger?"

"I heard what's been happening to you. We're sorry, all of us. Daddy's lawyer says we should never contact you again."

"That's good advice. Why are you ignoring it? Big brother may be listening in." He glanced around the parking lot. He was still alone.

"I need to see you. I have information you need."

"What kind of information?"

"Meet me and I'll tell you."

"That doesn't sound like a very smart thing to do."

"I'm in Clayton, New Mexico. At the Nite 'n Day Lodge. Come tomorrow, can you? I have some important information for you. About the Antelope Play."

How did she know about the Antelope Play? He thought a minute. "I'll try. If I'm not there by dark, I won't be coming. But I'll try."

"You won't regret it."

Back in Antelope City, Don glanced at a deed and vendor's lien note that Maye had prepared for a cousin of Elmer's who was buying a vacant lot in Borger. "That looks fine, Maye." He handed her the file. "Come out back. I want to show you something."

Maye followed him out the back door and away from the house. "What in the world?"

Quietly, Don said, "I need to go to Clayton. What's the best route?"

"You just go to Amarillo and head north. You'll be there in a couple of hours."

"I need an alternate route. One where there won't be many cars on the road. I want to know if I'm being followed."

"Followed?" She smiled. "The government man? So are we in trouble?"

"Maggie Shirls is in Clayton. She has some information for me. I don't want to lead the ATTF to her. Can I borrow your car? For all I know they've bugged mine."

"Of course you can. There's a back way to Dalhart. You'll know if anybody's trailing you. From there, you take State Highway 102. I think it becomes New Mexico 421, something like that. There's nothing out there." She looked around the backyard. "You think they've bugged the office? This is so exciting!"

"Who knows? Just be careful what you say." He opened the door for her.

"I'll get somebody out to repair that fence right away, Mr. Cuinn," she said loudly. She winked at Don.

Good grief. She's having fun.

He followed Maye's directions, taking the farm-to-market road south out of Antelope City, making a wide swing to the east and then headed north, skirting Velda County entirely, and finally going west on a little used county road to Dalhart. He stopped a couple of times and looked behind him. If there was anyone there he couldn't see them.

The countryside leveled off the farther north he got, with only a few arroyos and outcroppings breaking up the miles and miles of range and farmland. The winter wheat was in and the corporate farms that spread out over the High Plains were readying for the planting season. He passed miles of irrigated fields, huge round circles where the sprinklers sprayed the soil with gallon upon gallon of precious water pumped from the Ogallala, thousands of feet beneath the surface. Grain elevators were visible from a dozen miles away, clustered together like lost skyscrapers. Huge metal sheds held giant equipment, being prepared for spring.

He knew almost at once that bringing Maye's Honda was a mistake. He was driving the only passenger car on the road. All the other vehicles he saw were the pick-up trucks bearing the logos of oil companies, corporate farms, and service companies that worked in one or the other industry. He did pass an occasional cattle truck, hauling stock to and from the feedlots and cattle ranches that occupied about as much of the High Plains as did the farmers. In Maye's car, he was as noticeable as a circus train coming to town.

He could see Dalhart ahead and there was no one behind him. He pulled out onto Highway 87 and drove through the town looking for Highway 102. There was traffic here, normal people taking the normal route to Raton and Colorado Springs. *This is silly. I could have been in Clayton an hour ago.* He stopped at a red light and a Texas Highway Patrol car pulled up beside him. He looked straight ahead and let the trooper go first through the green light. *Maybe not so silly.*

The town huddled beside the busy highway, first new Dalhart with the Sonic Drive-In and Wal-Mart and three or four new down-market motels. There were a dozen gas stations in six blocks. Past the red light was old Dalhart, with empty brick buildings from the 1920s and '30s, a few repurposed as antique "shoppes." One or two housed relief agencies and labor halls where migrant workers could look for jobs in the fields, jobs that were all but gone now, replaced by the giant machines Don had seen on the way into town.

He breathed with relief when he found the road he was looking for, and again when he saw that it was empty. He headed northwest across the cultivated, but almost completely unpopulated, plains. A high peak stood sentry in the distance, and he knew he was in New Mexico when the sound of the road changed. He almost didn't notice the little sign welcoming him to the Land of Enchantment.

When he pulled into Clayton he had not seen a single car. The Nite 'n Day Lodge was the first motel he came to. Its parking lot was empty except for the graffiti-covered bus. Maggie must have been watching for him, because as soon as he parked, the door to a motel room flew open and she ran to the car.

"You came!" She threw her arms around him and kissed him. "Come in, come in. See my abode."

He disentangled himself and followed her into the motel room. The curtains were open and the bright sunlight exposed the shabbiness of the furniture and the need for a more thorough housekeeper. "Nice," he said. He closed the door and drew the curtains.

She sat on the bed, watching him. "Not the nicest in Clayton, I suppose, but it had a vacancy."

He took the only chair. "I'm not surprised."

"Would you like a Coke or something? There's a machine and ice right outside."

"No, I don't want a Coke. What am I doing here? What's this about the Antelope Play?"

"The Antelope Play and the Evergreen Plant. There's a connection there."

147

"Really. How do you know?"

"Hand me my backpack and I'll show you."

He found her bright red backpack on the floor next to the television and gave it to her. She rummaged through it, found an official looking folder and handed it to him.

"What's this?"

She smiled. "That is a report for the Nuclear Energy and Weapons Sub-Committee of the House Appropriations Committee. It lists the secret spending, the things that are never made public. Even in Congress, only the members of the Sub-Committee and the Chairman of the Appropriations Committee know what the individual items are."

Don opened the folder. "Classified."

"You betcha."

"How in the world did you get this?"

"I'm Maggie Shirls."

Don ran his finger down the list of projects. Someone had marked in red ink the projects for the Evergreen Weapons Plant. "So? I'm Don Cuinn."

"You don't know who my father is?" When he didn't answer, she went on. "Dan Shirls, Congressman from Colorado, and member of the Nuclear Energy and Weapons Sub-Committee."

"He didn't give you this," Don said flatly. His finger stopped at an item that read, "$50 million for Antelope Play Water Rights."

"My father is an unreconstructed and unrepentant liberal. He went to jail protesting the Vietnam War."

"And you are his daughter."

"He left this on his desk where he knew I would see it. He knows you're in Antelope City. He appreciates what you did for my friends and me. He knows about the trouble you're in for doing that. I think he believes this may help you, somehow."

Don closed the folder and gave it back to her.

"I made you a copy," she said.

"I don't want one," he said. "But I do appreciate the heads-up." *Now I need to find out why the government is spending that kind of money to buy water rights, and why two of Velda's most prominent citizens are fronting the purchases.* He stood up. "Get that folder back where it belongs. Let's hope to hell you weren't followed down here."

"Do I get a real 'thank you'?" She lay back on the bed and smiled. "I think you owe me that." She fingered the buttons on her blouse. "Come on, I like older guys. Have some fun for once in your life."

Don realized with a start that to Maggie, he was old. It was the first time in his life that had happened. He was in his early thirties and to this girl he was old. *Old enough to know better.* "Tempting, Maggie, but no. Button up and go home."

He took the main roads back to Velda. The traffic was heavy. He got in the right lane and settled in at the speed limit. He did not want an encounter of any kind with the law. As he drove, he tried unsuccessfully to sort out what was going on. He slowed down in Amarillo for the five mile trek from the Dalhart highway to the Velda turnoff. To his right, saw the bank building with Sawbucks Banjo's offices in the distance. He thought of pulling in there, telling Banjo what he had learned, seeing what he made of it all.

That's a bad idea, he decided. First of all, in was unlikely that Banjo was there. More important, he sensed the information was too valuable to share

149

with anyone, especially Banjo, who would immediately put the knowledge to work. Banjo would find a way to make serious money out of the secret.

Trey taxied to the barn that served as a hanger on the Laredo ranch. As he feathered the props, he could see two cars waiting. That was unusual. He opened the cockpit door and lowered the gangways. One man came to the cockpit and motioned to two others who loaded suitcases onto the plane. He tapped Trey on the shoulder and pointed at the other car, a stretch Cadillac limo. The rock that always seemed to be in Trey's stomach grew heavier. He opened the car door and looked inside.

"Get in." The voice came from a large shape in the corner of the backseat. *Doble Venganza*, smoking a cigar.

Trey sat in the jump seat across from the drug lord. "Surprised to see you here, *Doble*."

"It is not my preference," he said in precise English. "You have my Scotch?"

"Of course. A full case."

"Next trip bring four cases. *Ojos Tortuga* is getting married. There will be a celebration."

"No problem."

"I suppose not. But the other matter, we do have a problem."

"It's in process, *Doble*. I just need a little more time."

The drug lord blew cigar smoke in Trey's direction. "No more time. The next time I hear from you, it will be to say that you have my money."

"But *Doble* ..."

"No. Next time, my money."

It was unfair, but Trey knew better than to argue. He had seen himself what the *Venganza* cartel did to its enemies.

It happened at the cartel's headquarters in the mountains outside Acapulco. *Doble* and his lieutenants had a party to celebrate the purchase of the Laredo bank, a deal that Trey had arranged with cartel money. In the middle of the festivities, informers were dragged in. Their blindfolds were taken off and they were disemboweled. *Doble* ordered the executioners to take the bodies to their village. It would be a warning to anyone who might betray the cartel. *Doble* told Trey it was a coincidence the unfortunate event had to happen while he was there, but Trey knew that with *Doble Venganza* there were no coincidences.

What Trey couldn't understand was how fast the money had evaporated. He had used some of it to repay gambling debts in Las Vegas. Some went to replace that first series of "loans" he had made himself from the Pervoy family trust. The rest went to buy the Laredo ranch, land that *Doble* insisted he buy. Trey suspected that the land had already belonged to the cartel in one fashion or another

He could probably have worked through all that. The Laredo ranch was marketable. There was the possibility of an oil and gas lease. He might have a winning streak. God knows he deserved one. But there was no way he could have foreseen the failure of the Laredo bank. When it was closed by the banking authorities, the stock Trey had transferred to the cartel's U.S.

front became worthless and *Doble Venganza's* plan to use it for money laundering vanished. Now, he wanted his money back, all twenty million dollars, and Trey did not have it. He had already depleted the family trust. He had borrowed all he could from Velda and Amarillo banks. His wife and her money were locked up in Oklahoma, out of his reach. The water rights were his last hope.

"I understand," he said to *Doble Venganza*. "Four cases?"

"Make it six."

CHAPTER NINETEEN

It was mid-morning when Don got to his old office in the Han-Ro Building. Jake was not there.

"He's gone to the Pervoys to meet with Trey."

Don shook his head. "Tough meeting." He handed Faye the water rights agreements. "Have Jake call me if there's a problem." There was a stipulation, agreeing that the trustee could sell the water rights beneath the Pervoy Ranch. There was the resignation as trustee for Trey to sign. There was an agreement for all the living beneficiaries of the trust that Eugene was to be appointed substitute trustee.

Getting Eugene to agree hadn't been easy. "Are you joking me?" he had asked. An hour later he said, "You are joking me."

But Ginelle convinced him. "It's for the good of the family. Don Cuinn and Mr. Rosen will help you. I will help you. You have to do it, Hon."

He shook his head sorrowfully, but he signed the papers.

Faye thumbed through the documents. "I'm sure you got it just as you and Mr. Rosen agreed."

Don smiled. "Maye is almost as good a drafter of legal documents as you are."

"Does she ever mention she worked for the largest law firm in Amarillo?"

"It has come up."

Bridget opened the door to the law office. Her red hair was a little wind-blown. She brushed it back from her eyes. "Can I ask you something?"

"I was just coming to see you." He took her by the hand. "Let's go in here, where we can talk." He winked at Faye and led the girl into his old office.

155

Faye had cleaned it out completely. They stood by the window, looking at a spring day in Velda. He could make out traces of green beginning to appear on the landscape. The flag atop the courthouse flapped in a steady breeze from the southwest. "You first."

"No. I'm embarrassed," she said. "What was it you wanted to ask me?" Her pale skin was flushed.

"O.K., here goes. I've seen something, I can't tell you what, that makes me believe the government is funding the Antelope Play. The Antelope Play is..." he started to explain.

"I know what the Antelope Play is." She touched his arm. "The government? Our government? Is funding the water purchases?"

"Yep. The good old U.S. of A."

"But why?"

"I hoped you might know."

She thought for a minute. "Well, that might explain some things."

"What things?"

"Why the major has an Amarillo accounting firm doing all the accounting for the Antelope Play. That's the kind of thing I'd ordinarily handle. Why he brought in Hoppy Johnson, who he'd never used. Why he and Tommy Crackstone have been to Washington a half dozen times this year."

"So, any ideas?"

"No. Not one."

He leaned against the wall. Faye had had his office re-painted and new carpet laid. *Was his replacement on the way? Poor bastard.* "Well, it was worth a shot. Now, what did you want to ask me?"

"Tennis," she said. "Do you play tennis?"

156

"I used to. I haven't played since I moved up here. Why?"

"I thought you looked like a tennis player. If you're free Saturday, we're having a family project, getting our tennis court ready. If you don't mind a little work, I can promise you a match and a good dinner."

"You have a tennis court?"

"Doesn't everyone? If you're interested, come to the house about ten."

"I'll clear my busy calendar and see you then."

The O'Neill house was on Berry Boulevard, in the older part of Velda. He parked in front of the worn-looking two-story brick house of no distinguishable style. It had a porch around the front and down one side. A girl was standing at the porch corner, looking down into the adjacent lot, which was enclosed by a hedge.

He heard her call out, "You boyfriend's here, Bridey."

"Hush, Caitlin." Bridget came through an opening in the hedge and greeted him. She had on tennis shorts and a pullover. She pulled off the sweater and shook her red hair. "It's getting warm," she said. "This is my sister. Say hello to Mr. Cuinn, Caitlin."

She was taller than Bridget. She wore round glasses and had a girlish face. She had on a pair of sweats and an oversized jersey. She could have been thirty, she could have been forty, Don couldn't tell. He reached up over the railing and extended his hand. "Hello, I'm Don."

She looked at Bridget, who said, "Shake Don's hand, Caitlin."

157

Caitlin touched Don's outstretched hand briefly. She giggled. "You're Bridey's boyfriend."

"That's enough of that," Bridget said. She turned to Don. "Caitlin is going to make us all some iced tea and bring it down to the tennis court. Use the plastic glasses I set out, Caitlin, and bring lots of ice."

Caitlin smiled at Don. He winked at her, and she giggled again and went into the house.

"She seems like a very sweet person," Don said to Bridget.

"Yes," Bridget said. "She's had development problems, of course, but she's a joy. I love her very much."

On the other side of the hedge, two men were on their knees, pulling weeds from the red clay tennis court.

"Wow," Don said. "You do have your own tennis court."

"We do. But it's such a pain to get in shape each spring that I have to waylay unsuspecting newcomers as forced labor."

Three stacks of bags of fast-dry red clay were piled next to a drag broom and an old two-foot hand roller. A new net and new line tape were in their bags beside an ancient line stretcher. A carton of nails and two hammers were lying on a faded teak bench. The men waved and continued pulling weeds.

She touched his arm. "You know George of course."

Don waved at the older Poppoppolus brother, who grunted a greeting and then attacked a particularly stubborn weed.

The other man stood up and extended his hand. "I'm Marcas, Bridget's brother." Marcas was

158

redheaded and freckled, but with a lighter shade of red hair and more freckles than his sister. He was short, but built like a fireplug. His biceps strained under his tight-fitting t-shirt. "Bridget says you're a tennis player." He handed Don a weeder. "When we get this done, we can have a match."

"I haven't played in a long time."

"Excuses, excuses," Marcas said good-naturedly. "Figures. She said you were a Texas University tea-sipper."

It took an hour of vigorous digging by the four of them to rid the court of weeds. Don felt his muscles rebel at the stooping. *I haven't been working out enough.* After a short break for iced tea, they emptied the red clay onto the court, ready to be spread. When they had finished, Bridget called a break for lunch. They retreated, panting, to the porch, where Caitlin stood over plates of cheese and ham sandwiches.

They settled in, eating noisily. "Beer! For God's sake, beer!" George demanded. Marcas manhandled a large cooler from inside and handed them each an ice cold Shiner Bock.

Don took a long drink from his bottle. "God, that's good." He clicked bottles with Bridget. "Is this the only private tennis court in Velda?"

"It is," she answered.

"And it's yours."

"Yes it is."

He raised his eyebrows.

"This is the old Hansard house. The major was raised here."

"Somehow I can't see the major playing tennis."

She laughed. "The major? No. Apparently his father, the old colonel, built it for his son, but it was

159

never used. When the major moved to the penthouse, he gave the house to my mother. That was twenty-five years ago. All three of us learned to play on this court. My father taught us, before he...went away."

Quite a gift, Don started to say, then thought better of it. *Major Hansard and Bridget's mother, that is none of my business.*

They spent the rest of the afternoon spreading red clay onto the courts. They took turns pulling the creaky roller.

"That looks pretty level to me," Marcas said, wiping his brow with a muscled forearm.

George disagreed. "It's not nearly smooth. Look there. And there." He pointed at opposite ends of the court. "You like it uneven. It gives you a home court advantage."

"You'll never get over that, will you?" Marcas said. He grabbed the drag broom.

Bridget laughed. "Two years ago, George discovered that we put the tapes down wrong. The south end of the court was six inches longer than the north end. Marcas beat him four times before George realized what had happened."

George shook his finger at Marcas. "You knew. You practiced out here every day. You had to know."

Marcas laughed. "I never knew. I'm just more adaptable than you."

George pulled the roller over one of the suspect spots. "Adaptable? Yeah, that's one of your strong suits. Ask that union leader at Mineola."

Don looked at Bridget. "What?"

She got the line tape out of its bag and started measuring for the center. "Marcas is in Crackstone's labor relations department. They had a strike at the

160

Mineola Plant. The strikers tried to block the entrance to the plant and keep management from going inside. Marcas was in the plant manager's car. He got a little carried away. He knocked out the union president and chased off a dozen strikers. It didn't help that Marcas was an intercollegiate middleweight boxing champion."

"He called me a management son-of-a-bitch. I don't put up with that," Marcas said, pulling the drag broom vigorously.

"Then what happened?" Don asked.

"The company threw me to the wolves, that's what happened. Tommy Crackstone's a pussy."

Bridget handed one end of the line tape to Don and they started laying it out. "The union filed an unfair labor practice charge. The company agreed to suspend Marcas for six weeks and to restrict him from any labor dispute sites."

"That's harsh," Don said.

"Damn right it's harsh. And wrong." Marcas was red in the face. "If we ever have another strike, I have to sit it out, in the office, like some pariah." He squatted down and looked at the court. "Even enough for you?"

George nodded. "I suppose it'll have to do. Just don't touch those lines. I don't trust you." He oversaw the nailing in of the lines and the installation of the net.

Bridget looked at the sun, which was disappearing fast behind the trees. "There's still time for some doubles."

"Bridget and I will take on you two," George said to Marcas. George had not spoken directly to Don all day.

Bridget handed Don his racket. "Don is the newcomer. He and I will play you."

161

"Promise to be kind," Don said.

They weren't. Marcas slammed every shot at his sister, and George hit every ball directly at Don. Don and Bridget lost in straight sets.

George packed up and left without speaking. Bridget looked at Don, who was knocking the red clay off his shoes. "I've never seen George act like that." She turned to her brother. "I expect that kind of tennis from you, but not from George. He's usually a good sport."

"It's O.K.," Don said. "I'm sorry I couldn't play better."

"No, it's not. It's as if he wanted to kill you every time he hit the ball. I don't know what got into him."

"Don't you really?" Marcas said. "Are you really that clueless?"

"What do you mean?... Oh...He's jealous?... Of Don?"

"Of course he's jealous. I guess he thought you and he had some kind of understanding."

Bridget's white cheeks reddened. "We don't. Why would he think that?"

Don stood up and collected his things. "I thought I'd lost my natural charm."

"Don't go," she said, putting her hand on his arm. "There's something I want to show you." She turned back to her brother. "It makes me so angry. What right does he have to act that way?"

"You don't think you led him on, ever since his brother's wedding?"

"I certainly have not." She took Don's hand. "Come inside."

He followed her into the house. Bridget led him past a den where Caitlin sat watching television, into a room Bridget apparently used as a home

162

office. On the desk were a laptop computer and an expanding file folder.

He picked up a small statue of a nude boy from her desk. "Greek?"

"Yes. George brought it to me when he went back to their village for Tiny's wedding."

"I think I met Tiny's Greek wife once. She seems nice."

"She is. It was arranged, you know. Tiny's family found him a good wife. She's been wonderful for him."

"And George?"

"His family offered to find him someone too. He turned down the offer. He told them he could find his own wife."

"That would be you?"

"He may have thought so, once. But I've told him he needs someone different from me."

"Different in what way?"

"Well, someone who loves him, for one thing."

"That does help."

"Yes, it does." She handed him the red file. "Something you said reminded me of this."

"What is it?"

"Notes the old colonel made for a book he never wrote. It's a history of Velda County. I hadn't looked at it for years. Notice the part I clipped."

He took out a thick binder of typewritten pages, faded with age. Bridget had marked a section titled "Evergreen Plant Site Acquisition." It read:

Shortly after the end of the war, Charles Crackstone came down on the Super Chief from Boston to visit me. When he arrived, he asked if he could speak to me in complete confidence. I told him that of course he should feel free to do so. He told me that the War Department was planning to convert the Evergreen cannon plant into a top secret facility for the assembly of nuclear weapons, and that of course it needed much more land for that kind of facility than it now owned. For obvious national defense reasons, the War Department and the atomic energy section wanted this project to proceed with as little publicity as possible.

    Charles Crackstone serves on the Nuclear Weapons Advisory Board, and what with his commercial ties to the area, he was asked to help. His proposal was that he and I purchase the land needed for the new facility, hold it in trust for the government, and transfer it as needed, as unobtrusively as possible. No one would be surprised at our involvement, and we would use the explanation that Crackstone Industries was considering an expansion in the area (which was true) and needed the assurance that the land would be available. The eventual transfer to the government would be explained, if need be, as simply a change in Crackstone's plans that coincided with the government's needs. I of course agreed at once and we were able to secure the needed land, using our own agents. The government reimbursed us for the outlays for the land, and Secretary Stimson wrote us commendatory letters, saying that the government could never have acquired the property so quickly or so cheaply.

    Charles Crackstone later confided to me that during the Cuban missile crisis in the 1960s, he was called on for help again, this time acquiring, through a trading company, a small

island near Cuba from which Voice of America
broadcasts were made to Cuba, and from which
the Bay of Pigs invasion was directed. He also
said that though the invasion was a regrettable
failure, the purchase of the island itself was a
financial success, due to the large deposits of bird
guano that his company was able to mine
commercially. "Even guano can have a silver
lining," he said, although he did not use the word
'guano.'

"Well." Don said. "What do you make of that?"

"It's quite a coincidence, don't you think,
that the son of Colonel Hansard and the grandson
of Charles Crackstone are buying up water rights
near the Evergreen Plant?"

"It's more than a coincidence. I've learned
that the government is funding the water
purchases."

"Really?"

He told her about his road trip to Clayton
and Maggie Shirls's information. "I need to digest
all this. But thank you so much."

"You're welcome." She stood on tiptoes and
kissed him. "You're also welcome to spend the
night if you want to."

He felt a stirring, remembering her naked
in the moonlight at the cabin. "I wish I could. But I
just can't. Not yet."

"Does that mean, maybe sometime?"

"It doesn't mean anything." He took her
head in his hands and stared into her eyes.
"Bridget, don't wait around for me. I'm too messed
up for any girl, especially one as special as you."

165

"Ask me out to your place for dinner," she said. "Next weekend, maybe." She stroked his cheek. "You do owe me a dinner."

"I'll call you," he said.

"I wish I believed you."

By the time he got back to Antelope City, Don had decided what he needed to do. "Call Hoppy Johnson and tell him I need to meet with Tommy Crackstone right away."

He was waiting for Hoppy to set up the meeting when Elmer called. "Hey, Lawyer Cuinn. This is your faithful client Elmer Thorpe."

"I'd never have guessed. What can I do for you?"

"You know them water rights?"

"I believe that I do."

"I've decided to sell them. I told that landman to send the papers to you."

Don cursed to himself. "Hoppy Johnson? Hoppy Johnson called you direct?" *Hoppy had specifically agreed with Don to run everything through the law office, not bother Elmer.*

"Well, he didn't exactly call."

"So what exactly did he do?"

"He showed up here yesterday."

"In Vegas?"

"I think that's where we are."

Calm down. "What did he say?"

Don could hear Elmer talking to someone. "He wants to know what that landman said."

Lou Jo's voice was unmistakable, even from Nevada. "Well, tell him, you old fool."

Don waited, dreading what was coming.

"O.K. Here goes."

There was another long pause, followed by an old man's troubled wheeze.

"Hoppy Whatsisname said you were in trouble with the *federales*."

"What kind of trouble, did he say?"

"Something about hiding terrorists. I told him that was bullshit. Where would you hide 'em? In the shed out back? If you put any A-rab terrorists back there, they'd be froze by now."

"You're right about that."

"You didn't, did you?"

"Yes, Elmer. I'm hiding six suicide bombers in the shed, waiting for a chance to blow up that Antelope statue you had me spend three thousand dollars to restore."

"Anyway," Elmer went on, "Hop-a-Long says that your troubles would go away if Major Hansard and Tommy Crackstone sign some paper."

"Yes?"

"And that they would be more than willing to do that if I would be more flexible."

"He actually said more flexible?"

"That's what he said, wasn't it, Lou Jo?"

"Give me the phone, Elmer. You'll never get to the point."

Don could hear scuffling and a glass breaking. "That's my Bloody Mary, you damn witch."

"Lawyer Cuinn? This is Lou Jo."

"How're you today, Mrs. Thorpe?"

"As well as anybody could be, living with a man named Elmer Thorpe. Anyhow, the landman wanted us to sell the water rights. He even increased his offer to three and a half million. So it's not killing us to do it. And if it helps you, well so much the better."

167

"It's blackmail, and I don't like blackmail. Especially when they have got the government to help them do it."

More scuffling. "This here is Elmer again."

"You shouldn't do this, Elmer. You said you wanted to keep your water rights. You can't let them force you, especially on account of me."

"Listen to me, son. It's done. You hear me?"

"Yes sir. I hear you. What happened to coming back to Velda to live?"

"Oh, that. I don't think I want to come back. I don't like all this trouble. Lou Jo and I have our eyes on some sweet property outside of Austin. Some place they call Drip?"

"Dripping Springs?"

"I guess. Before you hang up. Lou Jo told you they're paying us another half a million? We figure that's because of your terrorist problem, whatever it is. So we're sending you half of that."

"No, no, no, no!"

But the Thorpes had hung up.

CHAPTER TWENTY

He followed Hoppy's directions to Tommy Crackstone's house. It was about ten miles north of Velda. "If you get to the Texas Gas pumping plant, you've gone too far."

The land was too broken by small caliche cliffs and dry creeks to be farmed. Its only value seemed to be the oil and gas wells that had been drilled every forty acres and the buried pipelines that rose out of the ground near the wells' production equipment. Small tanks, painted in the colors of their oil company owners, dotted the land as far as Don could see.

He found the gravel road with a bright red 'Private' sign and followed it cross-country another mile and a half. He saw no house, but he saw Hoppy's car parked in front of a large earthen mound. The skinny landman was standing by his car, smoking.

He signaled for Don to park next to him. "You found it," he said, when Don joined him.

"What the hell is this?" Don asked.

"The Crackstone Mansion. You've heard of the Crystal Palace. Well, this is the Earth Palace."

"What?"

"See for yourself. They're waiting for you down there." He pointed to a path and a barely visible tunnel entrance at its end.

"Did you say 'they'? Is the major here, too?"

"Hell, yes. Those two are like Siamese Twins. I've never met with one of them alone."

"They can wait. I'm not done with you, yet."

The landman grinned. "You got a problem?"

"You went to the Thorpes behind my back."

169

Hoppy shrugged. "I go where I'm sent. It was a very generous offer."

"Fuck off, Hoppy." He turned in disgust and walked down the flagstone path to the entrance. A large cypress door was ajar. "Hello?" he called.

"We're down here, Mr. Cuinn. Come in, please." Don recognized Crackstone's Boston Brahmin accent.

He went in slowly, letting his eyes adapt to the dark shadows. A few steps down and he was inside. Crackstone, slightly stooped, waited for him. He could make out a spacious anteroom and at one end, daylight. He followed Crackstone toward the daylight, trying not to bump into what must have been heavy wooden furniture. They came to a large atrium, lit by outside light streaming through skylights from high above.

Major Hansard sat on a stool by a large table, looking at a map. He glanced at Don and nodded.

Crackstone directed Don in, his hand outstretched. "Welcome to my bunker."

"Excuse me," Don said, "but what is this place?"

"A fair question. Actually, it was the home of my predecessor. When he left the company, we bought it from him."

"Not a big market in Velda for an underground house?"

"Not big, no. Too bad, because it's a fascinating place. It's completely underground, remarkably energy efficient. In fact, it uses no outside energy at all. We have solar panels, our own water well. The company has a renewable energy department and this is it."

"You don't live here?"

"God, no. Priscilla detests it. Not that it matters, she spends so little time in Velda. We have a place on Country Club Gulch."

"All above-ground."

"Indeed."

Don looked around. There were halls leading off in all directions. The house was huge.

The Major interrupted his inspection. "You told Mr. Johnson you wanted to talk to us?"

When Don got closer, the major leaned awkwardly over the table and tried to fold the map. He got his arm caught in the fold. "Help, Tommie, if you please." Crackstone rushed to his rescue, smiling to Don while he extricated the major, helped him back on his stool, then folded the map neatly and set it to one side.

Don waited until they were done and he had their attention. "I don't appreciate you sending Bustin Johns to threaten me."

"Bustin who? That's a remarkable name," Crackstone said.

Don bristled, remembering Crackstone's remarks about Don's own name the first time they met. "You're an expert on names, Mr. Crackstone. I'm sure you remember the name of the investigator with the Anti-Terrorism Task Force who called on me recently."

"You not still angry because I asked about the origin of your name, Mr. Cuinn? That was all in good fun. If I offended you, I'm terribly sorry."

Don couldn't tell whether Crackstone was sincere or not.

Hansard broke in, "Never mind all that. From what we're given to understand, the government is no longer interested in you. We gave them an endorsement of your good character. You should

171

thank us for that, rather than accusing us of God knows what."

Crackstone touched the major's arm. "On behalf of the Antelope Water Conservancy, we want to thank you. We now have Mr. Thorpe's water rights in hand, and we understand we will have the Pervoy Ranch water after the court hearing. Mr. Rosen says you have been a great help, and we thank you for that as well."

Don looked up at the skylights. "How tall is this ceiling?"

"What?" Crackstone replied. "I'm not sure. Twenty feet, maybe."

"Hmm. You may have Elmer Thorpe's rights, if I approve the papers, but you won't have the Pervoy Ranch until the new trustee is appointed and agrees to sell. The new trustee is also my client."

The major said, "I told you he would want money. How much?"

"Wait, Major. Let's hear him out. It isn't money you want, is it, Don? What is it you want?"

"I liked it better when you called me Cuinn."

"Excuse me. Of course."

"Let me tell you what I know. Then I'll tell you what more I want to know before I advise Eugene Pervoy to sell."

"Go right ahead, Mr. Cuinn." Crackstone sat in a chair next to the major's stool. They both stared at Don.

"For starters, I know that the government is funding the Antelope Play. I know the water rights are being acquired for the Evergreen Plant."

"But why would we . . ." Crackstone started to interrupt.

"Let me finish. I know that your father, Major, and your grandfather, Mr. Crackstone,

172

secretly bought the Evergreen plant site for the government. I think that you two are filling the same role for the water rights acquisition."

The two men exchanged glances. Hansard shrugged. "Suppose we are? I'm not saying that you're right, but even if you are, why does it make a difference?"

"It makes a difference because until I know why you're doing this, and by that I mean why the government wants the water rights, I have no way of knowing whether this is something my client ought to do."

""Suppose someone told you it was a matter of vital national interest?"

"What someone?"

"A high government official, perhaps someone knowledgeable about the Evergreen Plant?"

"Not good enough. I need to know what national interest? Are they thinking about expanding, starting to build weapons there? Are we getting ready for another arms race? I don't believe the Pervoys would want to be part of that."

"It's not that," Crackstone said. "I almost sure it is not that." He looked at the major. "Wait outside for a moment, will you?" Crackstone said. "The major and I need to talk."

He went outside. Hoppy Johnson had left and Don was glad. He was still too angry to have a civil discussion with the man.

In a few minutes, Crackstone appeared at the entrance to the tunnel and motioned for him to come back inside. "Let me show you something that you need to see."

"I can't wait."

Crackstone switched on the lights in the hall. On the wall there hung a large photograph of a man standing by an old-fashioned airplane on a rocky point by the sea. "That's Buckley Crackstone. He was too old to serve in World War I. So he bought his own plane, an old Bi-wing, learned to fly and flew submarine patrol on the New England coast, all at his own expense." He motioned for Don to go into the atrium. "So you see," he said, "there is a long tradition of service to the country in my family."

"And your grandfather helped arrange the Bay of Pigs invasion. Your family's selfless patriotism doesn't always work out, does it?"

"We disagree on that."

Back in the atrium, Major Hansard had moved to an easy chair. He sat with his short legs extended. He gave Don a withering stare.

Crackstone handed Don a card. "Go to the Evergreen entrance. This man is expecting you. He will answer your questions."

Don looked down at the card. It read, *Terry George, Director, Evergreen Facility*. "Now?"

"Do you know a better time?"

CHAPTER TWENTY-ONE

As soon as he was back on the highway, Don put the Bluetooth in his ear and checked in with Maye. "I'm going to meet a man named Terry George at the Evergreen Plant. Send the cops if you don't hear from me in three days."

"I hope you're joking again, Mr. Cuinn. I can never tell when you're joking."

"I'm joking, I'm joking. Anything important going on?"

"Let me see. You have some papers from Las Vegas here, with a sight draft for three and a half million dollars. And a personal check to you for two hundred and fifty thousand. Does that strike you as important?"

"Not really. Hold on to them. Wait. Look over the water rights agreements and see if they are the same as I reviewed before." He knew her review would be as thorough, in fact more thorough, than what he would do. "Is that it?"

"No. You had a strange call from Colorado."

"A female?" *Who knew who was listening, even if the major and Crackstone had vouched for his good character?*

"Yes. From Clayton." *Maggie. Maye was being careful too.*

"She asked me to tell you she had more information from her source."

Her father the Congressman. "Did she say what it was?"

"Yes. She said she had two words for you. One was Ogallala."

"What was the other one?"

"Contamination. I asked her to elaborate. She said she had to hurry, but she repeated those two words. 'Ogallala' and 'Contamination.'"

The guard at the Evergreen entrance didn't seem to think that Don was an honored guest. Don handed him his driver's license. "Mr. George is expecting me."

"Wait here, sir."

Don could see him talking into his phone inside the guardhouse. The last time he had seen him do that, an attack helicopter and the terrorist task force had appeared. Not this time.

"Get out of the vehicle, please."

Don watched the guard search his truck, including the toolbox in the bed that Don himself had never opened. It was good to see where the tools were.

"I need your cell phone, sir."

"My what?"

"Your phone. No visitor cell phones are allowed past this point."

"Why?" *He supposed it was because of cameras and recording devices. Maybe he could blow up the place with a cell phone.*

"I need your phone, and any other electronic devices."

"There's confidential material on there."

"I need your phone."

Don sighed. He snapped the back cover off his phone and removed the memory card, which he placed in his pocket. "Here you go," he said, handing the disabled camera to the guard, who put it in a plastic bag, sealed it and wrote Don's name across the bag with a flourish.

"Park in that lot over there. A guard will meet you and escort you to Mr. George's office."

The Evergreen administrative office was one of six identical two-story brick buildings that flanked a parking lot. In front of one building, an American flag on a thirty-foot pole flapped in the always-steady wind. Row upon row of small buildings, punctuated by a pair of massive structures, were barely visible in the distance. Otherwise, the land looked barren and unoccupied. The parking lot, however, was full except for several empty spaces marked "Visitors. Wait here for Escort."

An armed guard in full combat gear waited for him to park. "Follow me, please." Inside the administrative office, the guard left him in the reception area. There were government issue desks and chairs, long narrow halls and a set of double doors warning ominously, "No Admittance."

A heavy-set receptionist stared at a computer screen. Finally, she looked up and acknowledged Don's presence. Muttering to herself, she picked up her phone. "Mr. George," she said, "a man who says his name is Cuinn is here to see you."

In a few minutes, George, a lanky fifty-year old with unruly hair and a puzzled expression, came through the double doors. He shook Don's hand and motioned to a small conference room. "Let's go in here, Mr. Cuinn." The conference room was windowless and just large enough for a table and four chairs. "Mr. Crackstone asked me to speak to you. What is it I can tell you?"

"As you probably know, two of my clients have been asked to sell their water rights to something called the Antelope Water Conservancy."

"Yes?"

177

"Mr. Crackstone and Major Hansard are its public face, but just today I learned that the Antelope Water Conservancy is funded by the United States government and that the water rights purchase is for the benefit of the Evergreen Plant."

George took out a pen and wrote something on a yellow legal pad. He looked up at Don. "Where did you get this information?"

"I'm afraid I can't say."

"So you're guessing."

Don smiled. "No, I'm not. I'm here because Major Hansard and Tommy Crackstone sent me here. So we can agree that Evergreen is involved."

"If you believe that's true, what more do you want to know?"

"I did want to know why the government is involved. But now I believe I know why. I want you to confirm it."

George brushed his mop of hair out of his eyes. "Does your source know the penalty for dealing in classified information?"

Dom smiled tightly. "How much contamination has there been?"

"What are you talking about?"

"Contamination, of the greatest source of water on the High Plains, the Ogallala Aquiver. Isn't that what this is about? You guys have contaminated the Ogallala Aquiver with radioactive material and you're trying to hide it?"

"Oh, God," George said, "not water contamination again. Every time the anti-nuclear demonstrators try to shut us down, they claim we're polluting the water. Every time we investigate it, there's nothing to it. It's just old rumors, dragged out to scare people about Evergreen." George looked at his watch. "Here's the deal. During the 1950s, during the height of the Cold War, we were building nuclear weapons like crazy. The government needed an assembly plant. It needed to be in a fairly remote area, with no large population concentrations. This area was chosen and Evergreen was built."

"Remote, in case of an accident," Don interrupted.

"Yes," George answered, "but there was never an accident. Certainly nothing that ever went beyond the Evergreen boundaries."

"Are you still assembling weapons out here?" Don asked.

"No, of course not. After the Cold War ended, the treaties with the Russians called for the gradual elimination of existing weapons. So Evergreen turned around and started disassembling the weapons. That's the mission of Evergreen: the destruction of nuclear weapons. You'd think people would be in favor of that," he added defensively. "They seem to think we're not careful enough, that we've got nuclear materials at Evergreen that are going to escape somehow and kill people."

"And are they?"

George said gruffly, "No. Our safety record is impeccable. Our security is the highest level possible. We've never lost a milligram of any material."

"But you do store radioactive waste at Evergreen and theoretically it could get into the water supply, couldn't it?"

"No. Theoretically or factually, it has not and it could not."

"Then why are you buying water rights next to Evergreen?"

"You're not going to give up, are you?" When Don did not answer, he pulled a folder from a pile of

179

papers on the table. "This is your file, Mr. Cuinn. Everything the government knows about you. From your misadventures with the truth in Austin, to your troubles in Mexico, to your little escapade with the Colorado girls."

"I guess I should be surprised, but I'm not."

George turned a page in the file. "And how about this? We know about your trip to Clayton and we know that your source is Congressman Shirls' daughter."

Don had the sinking feeling George probably intended. *Don't say a word*, he reminded himself.

George slammed the folder shut. "But we also have the character references of two prominent Velda businessmen, men who might or might not be important to this agency. Our security check on you disclosed nothing that would indicate you're a security risk."

Don started to joke, then thought better of it. "Good. Because I'm not."

"I will tell you what you want to know, Mr. Cuinn, because I'm advised that doing so will expedite a project of vital interest to this facility."

Thank God! At last!

"But first, I need you to sign this." He slid a printed form across the table.

"What's this?"

"It's a 312. Or as you lawyers like to say, a Classified Information Nondisclosure Agreement."

"What does it say?"

"Read it, Counselor. Or do you need to get a lawyer to explain it to you?"

Don scanned the document. "So if you tell me something that's classified, I can't disclose it. If I do, I can be fined. Maybe put away."

"For up to ten years, that's right. Believe me, if I ever find out that you've disclosed what I'm about to tell you to anybody, including Congressman Shirls or his damn daughter, I'll be arguing for the max penalty."

"O.K., I get the picture."

George called in the heavy-set receptionist. Don scribbled his name to the document, as did George and the woman, who eyed Don suspiciously. When they were alone again, George said, "O.K. Let's start at the beginning. "Evergreen was built in the 1950s."

"On land bought for the government by Colonel Hansard and Tommy Crackstone's grandfather."

"Yes, yes. That's not even classified. Where to start? Do you know what a pit is, in a nuclear warhead?

"Not a clue. I was a history major."

George shook his head.

He thinks I'm a doofus.

George went on. "In a warhead, a plutonium pit is enclosed with detonators made of beryllium and plutonium. When the detonators are triggered, you get a wave of explosions. Without the exterior high explosives, a nuclear explosion can't take place, but deadly accidents can occur anyway. If the outer shell is breached, deadly radioactive material can escape into the atmosphere. Plutonium has a half-life of 22,500 years, so a radioactive spill can be deadly for over 100,000 years. Plutonium is one of the most deadly carcinogens known."

"O.K.," Don said. "It's dangerous over here. What's that got to do with the Antelope Play?"

"Bear with me, Counselor. Accidents have occurred in the past. Our biggest problem is

181

radioactive contamination. Test firing of high explosives from 1952 to 1984 was done at one of our firing sites, using depleted uranium and beryllium to simulate plutonium. Those tests contaminated the soil to a depth of nine inches with radioactive material. Burning of high explosives has contaminated soil in some locations on our east side maybe to 20 feet deep. Some contamination has reached a small local aquifer, but we are confident there has been no radioactive contamination of the Ogallala aquifer."

"How can you be sure?"

"We drilled monitoring wells all over the property to monitor the Ogallala for radioactive contamination. So far we haven't found contamination, but if there were to be any, it would be in the area along Evergreen's eastern boundary."

"Wait a minute. Are you really telling me that the federal government is spending tens of millions because there *might be* contamination?"

"I am."

"Excuse me if I'm a little skeptical. There has to be more to it than that."

"Listen," George said. Do you know how important the Ogallala Aquiver is?"

"I know it's big."

"The Ogallala is one of the world's largest aquifers. It covers an area of about 174,000 square miles in Nebraska, Wyoming, Colorado, Kansas, Oklahoma, New Mexico, and Texas. Nearly thirty percent of the irrigated land in the United States overlies it. It provides about 30 percent of the nation's ground water used for irrigation. It provides drinking water to three-fourths of the people who live within its boundary."

"Yes, I've read that."

182

"Can you imagine the danger to this country's economy if there was even a suspicion that the Ogallala Aquiver was contaminated? Can you imagine how difficult it would be to prove to all the people who drink water from the Ogallala or who eat crops irrigated with the Ogallala, that their water and their food is safe? Can you imagine what the outcry would be? What Congressman Shirls would do? It's unthinkable."

Don thought a minute. "I need to understand this. Explain why you need the water rights outside the Evergreen boundary if there isn't any contamination?"

"We need to drill more monitoring wells. We need to be absolutely sure that there hasn't been any contamination of the Ogallala Aquiver and that there never is."

"What happens if you do find contamination?"

"God help us. But at least we would know. We could track the progress, educate the public, I don't know what all. That's for someone smarter than me. My job is to keep this whole issue under wraps and at the same time make sure that the Ogallala is completely safe."

"And your job is also to co-opt me into helping you."

George got up. "Have I succeeded?"

Don didn't answer, but he said to himself, *Jesus, I guess he has.*

George opened the door. "I hope I have."

Don had just retrieved his cell phone and left Evergreen when the phone rang. He glanced at the screen, trying to hold the car in the road against the wind, which was blowing harder. It was Maggie. He disconnected her. *He was her lawyer. He could keep her secrets. But she couldn't keep his.*

He called and asked Jake to meet him at the Greeks. He parked in front and went in. Tiny waved at him and pointed to the back. George saw him but did not speak. *Still angry. Understandable.*

Jake was waiting in the small room where they had met before. "It's on you today. I hear you got a big payday from Elmer Thorpe."

"Are there no secrets?"

"Not in Velda. Or Amarillo either. The check was deposited this morning, I'm told. I got a call from your banker over there, asking about you."

"I told Maye to hold that check."

"Good luck telling her anything. I told her sister not to give you all that expensive furniture. Maybe you'll pay me for it now."

"Excuse me? Expensive? Do you want it back?"

Tiny appeared with a pitcher of beer and took their orders. "Where's George?" Jake asked.

"Busy," Tiny said with a nod toward Don.

"Ah. The eternal triangle." When Tiny left, Jake asked, "How is the little red-head? Feisty as ever?"

"George is just mad because I beat him at tennis."

"You didn't."

"No, I didn't. I was lucky to escape with bruises around my head." They sipped their beers. Don looked around. They were alone. "Let me ask you. Have you signed a 312?"

"For Evergreen and its water issues?"

"Yes. So you have signed one."

Jake raised his eyebrows. "Have you?"

"I have. Today." Don said. "I guess that means we can talk about it."

"We're probably expected to. After all, we're delivering the missing pieces of the Antelope Play."

Tiny brought their chili dogs and fries and left. Don took a bite, then said, "Terry George says there's been absolutely no radioactive contamination of the Ogallala Aquiver. Do you believe him?"

Jake wiped some mustard and chili from his chin. "Absolutely. Certainly. Of course. Yes. I believe him." He drank some beer. "Do you?"

"I'm not sure," Don replied.

"Neither am I," Jake said.

CHAPTER TWENTY-TWO

He called Austin and asked his mother what he could prepare for dinner with Bridget. "Spare no expense. I'm rich."

"There's a girl? I'm so glad, Donnie Ray," Dorrie Louise said.

"She's just a friend, Mama. I promised to cook dinner for her."

"If you are cooking, she's more than a friend. Anyway, here's what I would suggest."

He sent Maye to Market Street in Amarillo to pick up the ingredients on Dorrie Louise's list and he went back to Wal-Mart to buy a slow cooker. He even bought a matching set of inexpensive pottery and a couple of wine glasses.

After four hours in the crock pot, the pork shoulder, seasoned with cilantro and onions and lots of pepper was producing an aroma that Don remembered from his mother's kitchen in Smithberg. He had a green salad ready to toss with vinegar and oil, and water simmering for the brown rice. The rolls that Maye had baked were wrapped in foil ready to be heated in the Thorpes' old propane "Quality" range, which was purring contentedly, seemingly happy to be of use again. Maye had polished the porcelain and the striated marble edges and top. The old stove glistened like new.

Don poured himself a glass of the pinot noir he had found on a bottom shelf at the wine store in Amarillo. He had bought four bottles.

Maye packed her satchel-sized purse and looked at the table.

"Everything looks really nice, Maye," he said. "Thanks." He handed her a bottle of the wine. "Open this when you get home."

"I will certainly do that, Mr. Cuinn," Maye said. She adjusted one of the cream colored plates and smoothed the white tablecloth she had brought for him to use on the conference table. "You two have a nice dinner now."

Maye had just left when he saw Bridget's Corolla park in front of the store. He walked out the door to greet the redheaded girl. "Is that a new dent in your car?" he asked.

"Don't even mention it. I have to stop parking next to the major. He's half blind. He can barely see over the steering wheel and he scrapes my poor car almost every day."

"Doesn't he notice?"

"Well, his hearing's not so good either." She was carrying yellow roses in a vase. "From our garden. I'll put them in some water."

Don followed her into the office.

"What's that wonderful smell?" She ran some water in the vase and put the flowers on the table between the two place settings. "Maye's been at work here."

"How can you tell?" He handed her a glass of wine and she sat on a stool in the kitchen and watched him finish cooking. "It's a slow-cooked pork shoulder. A Hill Country recipe my mother taught me."

"Bless her," she said, sipping the wine.

He put the food on the table. She leaned over her food, inhaling the pork's fragrance before attacking the meal. He watched her eat, enjoying the way she talked and ate at the same time without a hint of awkwardness.

188

"Are these old family recipes? I mean, did your mother learn them from her mother?"

He poured them both some more wine. "I think she learned them from my step-mother, Lena. She worked in Lena's café when I was little."

"And your mother's family? What about them?"

"Is it sharing time?" When she didn't reply, he went on. "My mother got pregnant. Her folks kicked her out. Lena took us in, then raised me when Mama Louise married that son-of-a-bitch Grover. He wasn't too eager to get a stepson as part of the deal, and Lena wanted me. She and Papa never had a child."

"God, that's a sad story."

"Oh, it's not so sad. Lena and Papa raised me, loved me, sent me to U.T., did everything for me. And Mama loved me. She just felt she needed a husband, even if it came with a life in the sticks running Grover's café. That son-of-a-bitch."

"You're repeating yourself."

He stood up and began to clear the table. "No, sit there," he said when she started to help. "Pour us some more wine. One good secret deserves another."

She ran a long finger around the edge of her wine glass. "You know most of it. Father left. Mother got a job as the town millionaire's housekeeper. Millionaire takes on her whole family. He paid for our college, paid Caitlin's medical bills, got Marcas out of trouble a dozen times, got him the job at Crackstone. The major has meant everything to my family."

"So he thinks of you as his daughter?"

"More or less. Oh, people think it's more than that, but of course it isn't. I'd do anything in the world for him and I guess it shows."

She turned on the hot water and started washing the dishes.

"Leave those."

"For Maye to clean up? Not on your life. Grab a dishtowel and help. It won't take long."

As they worked he joked with her. "What's it like being a redhead? Do they have as much fun as blondes?"

She smiled. "For as long as I can remember, I've been dealing with this strange sort of attention. When I started kindergarten, and the kids saw my dark-haired mother, the first question out of their mouths was, 'Are you adopted?' By the time I made it to the sixth grade, I was confronted with a new theory: redheads were messengers of Satan. This was in parochial school. For all I know, the nuns believed it too. Redheads work for the devil. That's why their hair is red!"

"Was that bad or good?"

"It gave me a certain fame, I guess. But the real fun came later. Puberty was bad enough, but there were the boys who wanted to know if the carpet matched the curtains. When I figured out what they were talking about, I turned Marcas loose on them. And at confirmation, the priest whispered in my ear, "Never dye your hair.""

"You never did?"

"Not with God's representative on earth telling me not to, no, I did not. Actually, I love being a redhead. It's something only one or two percent of the human race can relate to." She looked around the kitchen. "This ought to pass inspection."

"It looks perfect to me. Thank you."

190

She stood on her tiptoes and kissed him. "No, thank you for the dinner. And the wine. I had so much wine, I wonder if I should drive?"

She's waiting for the invitation. "You can stay. In fact, you probably should stay."

She smiled. "Well, I did pack an overnight bag. It's in the car."

He brought in her bag. The wind blew the door shut behind him. He took the bag into the bedroom and pulled down the sheets. He had remade the bed that morning and the sheets were fresh. He picked up his pillow and an extra blanket. She stood in the doorway, watching. "I think you'll be comfortable." He held up his pillow. "I'll sleep on the couch in my office."

"I don't like to sleep alone in a strange bed."

"Bridget . . . I'm not ready for this."

"Because of your wife?"

He nodded.

"Can't you tell me what happened?"

He didn't answer, trying to decide what to say.

"Don," she said softly. "Tell me. It'll make it better, I promise."

"No, it won't."

"Please. Tell me."

She stroked his cheek, but he brushed her hand away. "I don't think I can."

"You can. You need to, don't you see?"

He slumped down on the floor. She knelt beside him. She took his hands. They were shaking. "Tell me. Please. What happened?"

He sobbed as he told her. Told her about Cecilia and their life together in Mexico; told her about missing the plane; told her about seeing the dead bodies by the side of the road; seeing Cecilia's

191

beautiful body riddled with bullets, lying beside her dead father and brothers; told her about the little gun in her hand and how she must have died defending herself; told her about the guilt that had weighed on him ever since that day, the guilt for not being there, not helping, not dying with her, which is what should have happened.

"There's nothing you could have done,"

"Yes, there is," he said. "I could have died."

She held him in her arms and stroked his head. "Come to bed with me. Let me hold you. Nothing more. Just let me hold you."

At last he slept, curled up against her.

CHAPTER TWENTY-THREE

He was alone in bed when the phone woke him. He could hear Maye talking. "I'll give him the message, Mr. Rosen. As soon as he comes out of his meeting."

She tapped on the door. "Mr. Cuinn? I have coffee."

He pulled on some clothes, straightened the bed and opened the door. No sign of Bridget. *I wonder what time she left?* He took the coffee, nodded his thanks to Maye and sat down. "That was Jake?"

"He says it's very important that you call him back right away. He's at the Pervoy Ranch."

"Give me a minute." He gulped the coffee and went into the bathroom. He splashed water on his face and rubbed his head vigorously with a towel. "You might as well get him back, Maye, thank you."

She picked up the phone and dialed the number. "Did you have a nice dinner last night?" she asked as it rang.

"Very nice," he said, taking the phone.

The older lawyer's whiskey voice answered. "Client conference? Give me a break."

"I do have clients, Jake."

"If you can tear yourself away from them, which I expect you can, get your ass out here to Trey's house. He and I need to talk to you."

"This morning?"

"No, on Martin Luther King's birthday. Of course, this morning. And hurry." Jake hung up.

"Goodbye to you, also," Don said. He handed the phone back to Maye. "I guess I have a meeting out of the office," he said. "Cancel my appointments."

"That shouldn't take too long," she replied.

It was mid-morning before he got to the main entrance of the Pervoy Ranch. A cowboy stood by a pick-up truck. He was carrying an M-40 military sniper rifle. He motioned for Don to get out of his truck and stand away. Don did as he was told. The cowboy looked inside the truck and in the bed. "You Lawyer Cuinn?"

"Yes. Yes, I am."

The cowboy held his cell phone in one hand, all the time waving the rifle generally in Don's direction. "That lawyer is here," he said into the phone. "'kay."

"They're waiting for you at Trey's house. You know the way?" He opened the gate and waved Don through.

"I expect I can find it," Don said, climbing back into his truck.

"This road, second ranch road to the left, on top of the hill. Sum bitch of a place, all glass. The reflection'll blind you. You can't miss it."

Don leaned out the window. "Thanks. Just curious, but who are you guarding against, out here in the middle of nowhere?"

The cowboy lit a cigarette and grinned. "The boss man says don't let nobody in. So far you're the first person to come by and he says let you in. Go figure."

The second turnoff to the left was about two miles up the winding road. To the right was the road leading to Eugene's house. He wondered what Eugene was doing to prepare to run the Pervoy family business. Don drove across rolling sandy hills and across iron culverts that bridged dry gullies. He

194

guessed that when it rained these gullies were filled with torrents of water. He looked at the clear blue sky and was cheered a little by it. Here and there a lone tree leaned in front of the southwest wind. Oil well pump jacks and tanks were all neatly painted, the price of doing business on the Pervoy Ranch. The land where pipelines had been laid had been restored, probably to a condition better than when it had been disturbed. Cattle gathered in small groups as far as he could see, protected from the oil field equipment by well-maintained fences. *Jake has done a good job for this family,* Don thought.

At exactly two miles on his odometer, he reached the top of a hill and saw Trey's ranch house below him. Its glass walls spread out in three directions, sheltering a deep blue swimming pool. The water in the pool shone in the noon sun. The glass house itself reflected the endless spaces that surrounded it.

He parked in the large circular drive. Two gardeners at work in the long flowerbeds around the pool glanced at him. Steam billowed up from the heated water in the pool. A tall, blond woman in a bikini came out of the cabana. She had a terry cloth robe over her shoulders, but she didn't bother to close it over her nearly nude, certainly flawless body. She held a tall glass in her hand. He could hear the tinkle of the ice in the glass as he approached her. He tried not to stare, but it seemed to be expected. "I'm Don Cuinn."

"Are you?" she said coolly. "I am Sandra Merrick." She looked at him directly and Don felt she was setting a value on his hair that needed a cut, his Old Navy shirt, his blue jeans, his worn work boots, his unmanicured nails. It only took a second, but Don had never been so completely appraised in

195

his life. She waved the glass toward the house. "They're waiting for you inside. Through there."

The front hall was two stories, with tile floors and a massive abstract painting on one wall. The adjoining wall was glass, with a view of the canyon beyond. The falloff nearly gave him vertigo. Through a large doorway there was a huge living room with a massive fireplace and several groupings of leather furniture and chrome tables. He heard voices through a second door. "Hello," he called.

"In here." It was Jake's voice. Jake stood at the doorway of a room that was as different as could be imagined from the parts of the house that Don had already seen. It was paneled in darkly stained pecan wood. On the walls were mounted heads of moose and elk and antelope. Trey Pervoy sat sunken into a large leather chair, a whiskey glass in his hands, his eyes staring dully. They flickered briefly when Don entered.

A third man stood in front of the over-sized fireplace. He wore a clerical collar. His bald head and cherubic face went well with the collar. He extended his hand. "Mr. Cuinn, I don't think we've ever met. I'm Jerry Burton."

"Hello."

"Sad day, I fear," he replied.

Don knew who the Episcopal priest was, but he wasn't sure what Father Jerry was doing here.

Jake said, "You made it at last, I see."

"I was delayed by a man with an M-40."

"Trey thinks it's necessary. He's probably right." Jake took his arm. "Come in here. I need to speak to you, and then Trey wants to talk to you. Right, Trey?" He touched the rancher on the shoulder. "Right, Trey? You want to talk to Don Cuinn? Eugene's lawyer?"

196

Trey gave a small start. "Yeah, I do. But I want Father Jerry here too."

"I'm here, Trey," the priest said. "I'm here."

Jake led Don to a small office off the den. He sat behind Trey's desk and fiddled with a glass paperweight. "Trey's in trouble."

"At least he has someone to comfort him in his trouble."

"Father Jerry?"

"Well maybe. I was really referring to the nice lady I met by the pool."

"So you met Sandra. His side action. She's been here since Trey's wife left him. I asked him not to bring her out here. He could always go to Amarillo if he had to see her, but he wants her nearby."

"I'd heard he had a friend in Amarillo. She doesn't look like a trust officer."

"Unfortunately, I'm afraid the trust has been paying for extra-banking services."

"Does his wife know?"

"I'm sure Margaret suspected he had a girlfriend. She'd explode for sure if she knew she was staying in her house."

"Sleeping in her bed."

"The divorce will be tough enough without that. The Aspens can be a vindictive bunch, so I've heard."

"Then why did he bring her here?"

"Trey's afraid to leave the ranch."

"Afraid of what?"

"Trey has gotten himself in big trouble. He owes a lot of money to a Mexican drug cartel."

Don came to attention. He had thought the mess was just about a spoiled kid with gambling debts and an expensive mistress. That was bad enough. But this? "Really?"

Jake dropped the paperweight with a thud. "Really. He owes them money and the water rights sale is the only way he knows to get enough cash to pay them off. No matter how much I've argued, I can't get him to resign as trustee."

Don smiled tightly. "You don't expect us to sit by and let him drain the trust to pay off some drug dealers?"

"After you've heard him, maybe you can convince Eugene to go along."

"I seriously doubt I'd even try."

Jake stood. "Hear him out, and then decide."

Back with Trey and Father Jerry, Don said, "Start at the beginning, Trey. How did you get in this mess?"

Trey looked defeated. "I haven't slept in weeks. I don't know what to do."

Father Jerry spoke up. "Tell him everything, Trey. Just like you told me."

"Just for this room, right? You can't tell anybody?"

Don glanced at Jake and the priest. "I'm not his lawyer. How can I promise that?"

Jake answered. "These are still settlement negotiations, about the trust lawsuit, like before. You can agree not to disclose."

Not if I hear about a criminal act. But, he said "O.K." *It was like crossing your fingers behind your back.* "Go ahead."

"I've been thinking about it. It's really Margaret's fault."

Your wife forced you to get mixed up with a Mexican drug cartel? Give me a break! "How so?"

198

Trey held up his empty glass and Jake poured four fingers of Scotch in it. The rancher took a large gulp and then went on. "Have you got any idea how much this house cost? Over three million dollars."

"It's very nice," Don said.

"Nice, shit. I had to fly her out to that goddamned Frank Lloyd Wright's nephew's wife's cousin's place in Arizona. She'd stay days at a time, talking about this window, or that piece of handmade crap. It was too much. I tapped the trust for that, paid myself an advance distribution. I always intended to pay it back."

"At first I thought maybe she'd use some of her own money to help out, but no! Old man Aspen wouldn't turn loose a dime of Margaret's trust money for her own house. Her house! Finally I just said, what the shit. We'll get through it some way. So I would drop her off in Scottsdale, tell her to do whatever she wanted to, then I'd fly on out to Vegas."

"I was so mad at her, I thought, well, treat yourself. I had a standing reservation for a high rollers suite at the Venetian. I started playing blackjack at the big stake tables. Anything I wanted was comped. All I had to do was sign a chit when I lost."

"You never won?"

"Of course I won. Enough to fix everything, if I had just stopped. But I didn't. I guess I became addicted. That's possible, isn't it?"

"Of course it is," Father Jerry says. "I've seen it many times."

Sure you have. What you're seeing is the Pervoy fortune, that paid for your new manse and underwrites your salary, evaporate before your eyes. "Go on," Don said.

Trey emptied his glass again. He handed it to Father Jerry this time. The priest refilled it and poured himself a stiff drink as well. The chubby clergyman's forehead was wet with perspiration.

"I covered it at first," Trey said. "I used the money for the house. Then, I borrowed more from the trust. When there wasn't enough to cover the checks to Mama and Eugene and Mada, I went to a loan shark that the casino recommended. When I tapped out there, I was desperate."

"What did you do?"

Trey hesitated. He wiped his brow with a large linen handkerchief and didn't seem to notice when he dropped it on the floor. It fluttered like a white flag of surrender. "Like I said, I was desperate. The loan shark was pressing me. He said that he had a Mexican 'friend' who was looking for an American business associate. I should have known better, but what choice did I have?"

Yes, like you said, you were desperate.

"That's how I got involved with *Doble Venganza.*"

Don reached for the whiskey himself. "Did you say *Venganza?*"

"Yes. I don't know his real name. I called him *Doble.*"

"The *Venganza* drug cartel? That's who've got you in their clutches?"

"You know them?" Jake asked.

"I heard of them," Don answered. "When I lived in Mexico."

Trey seemed anxious to tell it all now. The story poured out like flood water ravaging the countryside.

"We met across the border from Laredo. He paid off my debts and loaned me money to buy the Laredo ranch from a shell company of his." He turned to Jake. "Remember, we agreed the trust could buy it as an investment, run cattle, maybe lease it for oil and gas?"

"I do," Jake answered. "You replaced trust money with the Mexican's money and then spent it on the Laredo ranch?"

"Yes. There were tunnels and cellars under the buildings and God knows what else. It already had an airstrip and pretty soon I was ferrying drugs between there and our place here."

"Jesus," Jake said. "How did you ever expect to get out of that?"

"He offered me a way. I fronted the purchase of that little bank in Laredo. Remember?"

"You told me that was your own money," Jake said.

"It was *Venganza* money. He had me setting up foreign accounts, transferring money to God knows where. It was too much for me, so I had Sandra work it from Amarillo. It all ran smooth as clockwork. But then . . ."

"The Feds," Jake said.

"The bank failed. Too many real estate loans. For some reason, the examiners never got around to the money transfers. They just shut the place down, transferred the assets, wrote off the losses. The investors got nothing."

"And *Doble Venganza* is not pleased," Don said.

"He wants his ten million back. Plus another ten he says I owe him for the ranch and for the Vegas loans. I've told him I didn't have it. He said, 'Sell something.' I tried to explain that the Ranch isn't mine to sell. I could tell he didn't believe me. But then . . ."

"The water rights offer . . ." Don said.

"It was a God-send. A way out. I could pay him off, maybe sell the Laredo ranch, pay distributions until I managed to pay back the money I took from the trust."

"Except you don't have authority to sell the water rights."

Tears ran down Trey's tanned face. He brushed them away with the sleeve of his shirt. "You have to convince Eugene. It's my only way out. Otherwise, I'm a dead man."

Don did not argue. With his own eyes, he had seen what the *Venganzas* were capable of doing. The roadside ambush, the dead bodies, Cecilia, flooded his memory and he couldn't speak.

"You saw me after they beat me," Trey said.

"The fall off a horse? I wondered about that. But this? I never dreamed."

"Worse, I was at *Doble's rancho*. I watched them rip the guts out of three informers. It was a warning to me. After that I didn't argue. I ferried cocaine up here and cartel members back and forth to Laredo. Along with cases of his favorite Scotch whiskey. I always had to deliver the Scotch. I guess it's hard to get in Mexico. That's where all the Scotch I got from you went," he said to Jake. "He even wants six cases for Turtle Eyes' wedding. Can you get me six cases?" he said to Jake with a little smile.

"Of course," Jake said. "Don't worry about the Scotch."

"Stay with Trey, will you?" Don said to Father Jerry. "Jake and I need to talk some more."

Don and Jake stood on the back patio. He could hear the leaf blowers going on the other side of the house. "I know these guys. They'll kill him and never look back."

Jake looked at him sharply. "You know them? How?"

Don sighed. He'd never told anyone what happened to Cecilia until he told Bridget. "They killed my wife, and her entire family. I know what they are capable of."

"My God! The whole family?" He hesitated, then asked, "What are we going to do?"

Don thought. "They want twenty million? They'll settle for less. Maybe five? Do we have five?"

"I can probably round it up, but Trey's in no condition to negotiate."

"You're right." He turned to go back in the house. "I'll do it."

"You're crazy. After what you told me. Won't they know who you are?"

"There's no reason they should. They weren't after Cecilia. She just happened to be in the wrong place when they ambushed her father."

Jake touched Don's sleeve. "Wait. I can't let you do this."

Don shrugged off the older man's hand. "I want to. I want to look my wife's murderer in the eyes."

"You're not going to try to do something, are you?"

"Like what?"

"Like get revenge?"

"If only I could."

CHAPTER TWENTY-FOUR

With a shaking hand, Trey signed the letter of resignation as trustee of the Pervoy Family Trust and his consent for Eugene to be his successor. "Do you really believe this will work?"

"I do believe that," Don said.

When they were alone, Don said to Jake. "You know he'll probably have to do federal time for the drug trafficking, when this is over?"

"I'll let him recover a little before I spring that on him. For now we have to find five million in trust assets."

"Do that. But I may not need it."

"Really? Why not?"

"There may be another source. A source with lots of ready cash."

He met Bustin Johns in the conference room at the Evergreen plant. It was the most secure place he knew.

"Tell me again why the ATTF should give you five million dollars?"

"Drug trafficking is part of your charter, isn't it?"

Johns nodded. "We do work closely with ATF."

"I can deliver you the routing number for the *Venganza* cartel. You should be able to track the flow of money and seize their assets, get your money back plus a lot more."

"Is that all? Some routing number?"

Don thought. "I can't divulge the name of my client, but he has been deeply involved in the cartel's stateside operations. I can deliver you the cartel's delivery channels. I can tell you the details of the cartel's involvement in a South Texas bank. I can tell you of a large ranch that the cartel owns, beneficially, and the name of the legal owner."

"And you want a deal for this client of yours?"

"Of course."

"Tell me what you know and we'll see where it leads us."

From the co-pilot's seat in Trey's Twin Beech Baron, Don watched the Panhandle landscape recede beneath them. He repeated the phone number one more time. It was the number at the First Ranchers Bank of Amarillo, where Johns and Sandra Merrick would be waiting for his call, ready to send five million dollars into the Ethernet, but especially coded so that the ATTF could track the money as it bounced around tax havens before finally coming to rest in the *Venganza's* home depository.

Don argued futilely for the government not to prosecute Trey, but the best he had been able to do was an agreement with the U.S. Attorney for a reduced sentence of three to five years in prison. He tried to explain to Trey he would not have to serve much more than a year, but the broken rancher just nodded mutely.

Don glanced at Trey, who was concentrating on setting his instruments for the flight down to the Laredo ranch. He seemed calmer now. He had even smiled a little when Don helped him load the six cases of Bladnoch on board. "If I can get them drunk enough, maybe I can cut a better deal."

"Don't count on that. They just get meaner when they drink."

Don watched the High Plains fade into the shadows. The engines droned quietly and the Baron rocked as it made way against the gentle headwinds. He fretted. No matter how he tried to rest, he was too nervous. It seemed forever, but finally, Trey lowered the flaps and the landing gear and they were on their approach. Lights flashed on and he could see the landing strip rise up to meet them.

Trey executed a perfect touchdown. He feathered the engines and taxied slowly to the barn. "There they are," he said. Men were waiting by the barn door.

Don opened the gangway and climbed down. A tall man approached. He was wearing black shirt and pants and a baseball cap. *"Señor Cuinn?"*

"Yes," Don answered.

"Tienes el dinero?"

Don decided that he would not speak Spanish to these people. The less they knew about him the better.

"The money. *Señor* Pervoy sent word that you were bringing the money. Do you have the money?"

"I have the transfer instructions."

"Give them to me."

"No. They are only for *Señor Doble Venganza* himself."

"To me. I'll give them to *El Jefe*."

"No. Only for *Doble Venganza*.

The man looked hard at Don. *"Buscar lo."* he said to one of his helpers. The man patted him down and said *"Él es O.K."*

Don could hear snippets of the Tall Man's phone call. He came back and said, "You will come with us." He gave rapid instructions to the other men and in a few minutes the Scotch had been unloaded and taken into the barn, replaced by suitcases for Trey to transport back to Velda. The Tall Man half-pulled him into the barn. Don tried to

207

speak a last time to Trey, but the Tall Man said, *"Prisa!* Hurry! This way!"

Inside, the barn was brightly lit. Crates were stacked in one corner. A table with coffee and half-eaten food was in another. In the center was an open trapdoor with steps, down which the men were passing the cases of Scotch. When they were done, the Tall Man motioned for Don to go down the stairs. At the bottom was a well-lit tunnel with a rail track and a small electric tram. The cement-lined tunnel was tall enough for the Tall Man to stand upright. They climbed on the tram, pressing against each other. Don could smell their sweat and sour breath. Large fans in the ceiling of the tunnel blew welcome cool air over them. The car sped along the tunnel, descending, then leveling off. Don supposed they were under the Rio Grande River. They ascended again and stopped at another set of stairs.

"Bienvenido a México," the Tall Man said.

Don grunted and followed the man up the stairs and outside into the darkness. A black SUV was waiting. The Tall Man shoved him in the back. A driver and another man were in the front. *"A El Jefe."* He slammed the door and slapped on the roof on the car, telling them in Spanish to hurry.

The guard in the front seat handed Don a black hood. "Put on," he said in broken English.

Don did as he was told and settled back in the seat and thought of the meeting ahead. He remembered the roadside where Cecilia lay dead. In his imagination, she brushed the blood off her face and smiled at him. "It's O.K., Donnie, *mi amor.* I shot the bastards, did you see?" After some hours, the car stopped with a jerk. The guard got out. In a few minutes he came back.

He pulled off Don's hood. They were in front of a non-descript roadside stand. He thrust a wrapped *torta* in Don's hands. Don ate the fried pork and grilled onions and peppers eagerly. He hadn't realized that he was hungry. When he was done, he pulled the hood back down over his head. The guard said something to the driver and the car started again.

When they stopped next, the guard pulled off the hood and opened the car door. The bright sunlight blinded him at first but then he could see they were on the side of the highway, at a rocky overlook. *"Mear,"* the guard told him.

The three men sent streams of piss down the cliff. The two Mexicans laughed and tried to outdo each other. The driver smiled at Don. "Thirsty?"

"Yes," Don replied, taking the bottle of water the man offered him. "Thanks."

From there, time passed even more slowly. Even with the hood over his head, Don could tell when they passed through towns, most of them seeming small. Eventually, the car stopped. A pair of hands pulled off the hood. Don blinked. Someone opened the car door and spoke to him. *"Sígame, por favor."* An attractive young woman, traditionally dressed, indicated that he should follow her. He got out of the car. He was in the middle of a sprawling compound. In a large courtyard, men were busy stringing lights on poles and in trees. Others were moving tables and benches. *That's where they killed the informers and made Trey watch*, he thought.

The girl led him to a cabin apart from the main house. Inside, she motioned to a bar, stocked with tequila, lime juice and ice. There was a neatly made bed and a tiled bathroom.

209

Don asked, "When will I see *Señor Venganza*?"

The girl smiled and said, *"Disculpe, sino que no hablo Inglés."*

He started to rephrase his question in Spanish, but caught himself. Before he could speak again, she was gone. He sat on the bed and tried to rehearse the upcoming negotiation. There was a tap on the door and a young boy handed him his duffle. Don opened it. The contents were jumbled and no attempt had been made to disguise that it had been searched. He decided to shower and change clothes.

He was putting on his shoes when the girl knocked on his door and motioned for him to follow her. She led him across the compound to the big house. The decoration of the courtyard seemed complete. Small groups of dark skinned men stared at Don as he and the girl crossed the drive to the main house. Don estimated there were fifty or sixty men in the compound. "A big wedding?"

"Wedding," she repeated slowly. She pointed down the hall. *"El Jefe es así.* Go There. *El Jefe."* Then she was gone again. He walked slowly down the dark hall. A candle lit a jeweled shrine to the Virgin. At the end of the hall, a man stood. He wore a heavy shirt and dull leather boots. He held a rifle. He stood aside, watching Don silently.

The room was an office. Stacks of papers with scribbled notes covered the work surface of an old fashioned roll-top desk. Across the room, a computer screen blinked on a large worktable. A middle-aged man with glasses sat in front of the computer. He glanced at Don, then returned to the screen. Through a door at the back of the room was a small, enclosed porch.

From the porch, a voice called, "Out here, *Señor* Cuinn. Join me."

On the porch, a man with dark hair and bronze skin sat in a wooden rocking chair. He was smoking a cigar. He held it with extremely long fingers. *Like a pianist.* Large embossed gold cufflinks decorated the cuffs of his heavily starched white shirt. *It was Doble Venganza. The ATTF's photos were accurate.* The cufflinks glittered. He tore his eyes away.

"Sit," *Doble* said.

Don could see the courtyard from the porch. The lights in the trees flickered in the fading light of the late afternoon. He sat down and waited.

"Do you prefer we proceed in English?" *Doble* said, with only a slight accent.

"Yes." Don answered. *He stared at the drug lord, imprinting his face in his memory. He tried to push away the memory of Cecilia. If he was to do this, he needed to focus now, more than ever in his life.*

"Mr. Pervoy did not send a bi-lingual lawyer to plead his case. That is too bad."

"He sent what he had, and that's just me, I'm afraid."

"No matter. We will use English. I want there to be no misunderstanding at all in what we speak of. Do you understand?"

"Mr. Pervoy wants no misunderstanding either."

Doble rattled his glass and the guard appeared with a bottle of whiskey. "A drink, perhaps, before we begin? This is some of Mr. Pervoy's excellent Scotch whiskey."

"I understand the cases he sent with me are of the finest vintage. But I always drink tequila in

211

Mexico, if that's not too much trouble." Before Don left, Bustin Johns had said to him, "Only drink tequila in Mexico." In fact, he had said it twice.

Doble nodded. "Of course. A guest should always have the best tequila." He looked up at the guard. *"El mejor tequila para el señor."* He looked at Don and smiled. "I told him to bring you the best we have."

"Thank you."

"Where did you go to law school, Mr. Cuinn?"

Don supposed the computer expert in the other room had already Googled Don and the drug lord knew almost everything about him. *Except that he killed my wife.* "A small school. Jeff Davis."

The guard returned with Don's drink. "That school I do not know."

"It is in southeast Texas."

"Of course. And somehow you found your way to the northernmost part of Texas? Why?"

"The same reason so many of your countrymen go north. To find work."

"Will there be new immigration laws, do you think?"

"I have no idea."

"Will drugs be legalized in your country?"

"No."

"That is good." He put down his glass and snapped his fingers. "Oscar, bring the accounting." He smiled at Don. "Oscar speaks perfect English. Many years working in California." The bookkeeper appeared at once. He handed *Doble* a sheet of paper. The cartel leader glanced at the paper and said, "According to our records, Mr. Pervoy is indebted to us in the amount of twenty million, four hundred thousand dollars. Has he sent you here with that amount?"

Don smiled. "I'm afraid not."

"Then why are you here?"

"To reach a settlement and end Mr. Pervoy's relationship with you and your associates, I hope."

Doble handed the paper back to Oscar, who scurried back to the office. "How much?"

"Five million."

"You joke. Less than twenty-five percent. That is insulting." His stare seemed intended to remind Don that *Doble Venganza* did not like to be insulted. "The entire amount. Or the consequences to your client will be unfortunate."

"It's all he has. There is no more."

"Nonsense. He owns a big *rancho*. Sell something."

"He does not own it. There is a trust. There are others in the family who share in it."

"He should tell his *familia* that he will die if he does not sell the *rancho*. That would persuade them, would it not?"

"No."

"No? Really?"

"There is no love lost in the Pervoy family."

"Ah. So the *gringo* who has cheated me has cheated his own family as well?"

"Those are your words, not mine."

Doble stared at the courtyard. "This week will be a fiesta here. My youngest brother is getting married." He turned to Don and smiled. "He is like a son to me. He will succeed me in this business when I die. You see, in this *familia,* there is no discord. Not like your countrymen."

"Then you are lucky."

Doble picked up a large Bowie knife from the table and flipped it in the air. It stuck into the wood surface. "A good sign. For your client. I will settle for ten million."

"And leave him alone?"

"Why not? In this business, one must change supply routes often. We will soon be using a different route to the Chicago market. *Señor* Pervoy's usefulness to us is over. The drug enforcers will find him soon. That will be the end of him. Perhaps his family will be pleased."

"I have a phone number to a bank in Amarillo. If I call that number, Mr. Pervoy's associate at the bank will answer."

"His whore?" *Doble* sneered.

"His very good friend. You are well-informed."

"*Señor* Pervoy owes me a great deal of money."

"His associate at the bank will transfer five million dollars according to your instructions. In thirty days, Oscar can call the same number, give her instructions, and she will transfer another five million."

"And the U.S. banking regulations? They prohibit these kinds of transfers, I believe."

It was Don's time to smile. "Mr. Pervoy's associate is not only beautiful, she is also very talented. The money will arrive."

"When will you make the call?"

"When I am safely back in the United States."

"A prudent man." The drug cartel leader rose. He looked at his starched cuff. "You admire my cufflinks? I saw you looking at them."

"They're unusual."

"A memento of a business affair." With a practiced motion, he freed them from his cuff and handed them to Don. "Take them, as a souvenir of our arrangement."

Don took the cuff links and quickly dropped them in his pocket. "You're very generous."

"With cuff links. Not with money."

CHAPTER TWENTY-FIVE

Don stood with Bridget at the edge of the crowd. All of Velda's leading citizens were there for the burial of the eldest son of the largest landowner in the county. Father Jerry motioned for the family to come to the graveside where the hovering owner of the Blackstone Funeral Home had placed chairs for the family. There were two places of honor, one for Trey's mother, back from Longview, where she had fled when Trey's affairs began to unravel, flown back to Velda in someone's private plane and ready to resume her duties as Velda's grande dame. The other was for Trey's widow, Margaret Aspen Pervoy. The two women sat next to each other in stony silence. Trey's children George IV, Quatro, and Mary Marie, Junior, stood behind their mother.

"I wonder if those nicknames will stick, back in Oklahoma," Don whispered to Bridget.

"Shh," she answered. Eugene and his family were sitting in the second row of chairs. Eugene looked uncomfortable in the tight collared white shirt and black suit. He waved weakly at Don. Ginelle had been to Neiman Marcus to buy herself a new dress, Maye had reported.

"Good for her," Don had replied.

Trey and Eugene's sister, the recently divorced Belle Mada, had been recalled from the Cote d'Azur and jet-lag from the long flight showed in her haggard face. Jake reported she had signed the water rights agreement with no fuss, only asking if her monthly checks were going to increase. Jake had told her they would not. "She didn't even blink when I told her Eugene is the new trustee. I think she's on something."

A gaggle of Aspens stood protectively behind Trey's widow and her children. Don supposed the marriage had ended better than they might have hoped. At least their daughter's money was untouched and her husband had died with only a whiff of scandal.

The familiar liturgy began.

At the ranch outside Laredo, Don had been met by the Tall Man, who watched carefully while Don placed the call to Amarillo.

Don hung up, and said, "It's done."

The Tall Man supervised his men as they arranged a final shipment of drugs for Trey to ferry back to Velda. Trey's plane was late. After an hour without word, and apparently sensing trouble, the Tall Man ordered his men to take the drugs back into the warehouse. He pointed Don toward town and turned off the lights.

The night stars were bright and there was a full moon. Don walked down the road until he was out of sight of the warehouse and called Jake in Velda.

"Are you all right? Where are you?"

"Yes, and in Laredo. More to the point, where's Trey?"

"He's dead."

"Dead? How? Those bastards didn't kill him, did they?"

"No. After he dropped you off, he took off without a flight plan. Apparently he set the controls on auto-pilot and took a bottle of sleeping pills. The plane flew itself until it ran out of gas and crashed. At least that's what the NTSB thinks happened. We've used all the political influence we and the

*Aspens have, and so far the feds are calling it
'equipment malfunction.'"*

*"Jesus. I made a deal with Doble. I think
Trey would have come out of it all right."*

"I guess he couldn't stand the disgrace."

Father Jerry was finishing. "...we commend to
Almighty God our brother George; and we commit
his body to the ground; earth to earth, ashes to
ashes, dust to dust. The Lord bless him and keep
him, the Lord make his face to smile upon him and
be gracious unto him, the Lord lift up his
countenance upon him and give him peace. Amen."

The Episcopal priest knelt beside the dead
man's mother and whispered in her ear. He turned
to his widow and embraced her. She thanked him
with a forced smile, then turned to her father, said
something, and in a second, all the Aspens,
including Trey's children, were gone.

Don and Bridget followed the crowd to the
rows of cars parked in the cemetery's narrow roads.
They got in her little car and followed the ragged
procession down Country Club Gulch to the Club for
the reception. As they left the cemetery, Don
thought he saw Bustin Johns standing some
distance away, with two men in black suits.
*Watching to see if there were any cartel members
here to strip poor Trey's corpse bare,* he supposed.
It was the first time he had thought of the dead man
as "poor Trey."

"That went well," Bridget said. She steered
into line behind the major's Mercedes. "Marcas is
driving the major."

"Lucky him." Don looked at the long line of
cars. "So what's the word? What are people saying?"

Bridget waved for an elderly woman in a big Cadillac to join the line ahead of them. "I think the town has silently agreed that Trey's death was accidental."

"But?"

"Well, it is Velda. I've already heard the rumors of suicide." She looked at Don and smiled. "The most popular theory is that he died of a broken heart. He couldn't live without Margaret Aspen."

"Yeah, that's the way I see it," Don said.

At the club, they stood in a long line to pay their respects to Trey's mother, who sat regally in a straight chair at the entrance to the dining room. Eugene and his family stood beside her, along with his wobbly sister. They shook hands stiffly with the long line of Veldanians.

When Don and Bridget reached the grieving mother, she said to Bridget under her breathe, "I never liked those Aspens. New money. Imagine not even coming to the reception. That daughter of theirs killed my poor son, drove him to kill himself. And now, whatever will they do to those poor children? God knows I hated to leave my friends in Longview, but it's my duty to come back here and assist my darling Eugene any way I can, and to help care for his dear children."

When they finally made it to the bar, Don said to Bridget, "Ginelle has a fight ahead of her. I wouldn't bet against her though. She's strong."

"Eugene's mother may have met her match," Bridget said.

Once more, Don met with Bustin Johns in the Evergreen conference room. Johns looked tired. "Tough day?" Don asked.

"Every day...' full of those events that alter and illuminate history.'"

"What's that from?"

"An old, old, TV show." He rubbed his eyes, cleaned his glasses and put them back on his thin nose. "So tell me. Everything."

Don relived his trip to the cartel's headquarters. Johns listened, interrupting now and then with a question. When Don had finished, Johns said, "The operation went well. We traced the money and, for some reason, we followed it quite easily, all the way to the *Venganza's* main account in the Caymans."

Don laid the cufflinks on the desk. The initial engraved on them was an "M". Johns looked at them and then at Don, who said, "My wife's brother's. They were his favorite pair. *Doble* gave them to me, to seal our deal."

"He'd want them back if he suspected we'd accessed all his cash." He smiled.

"How could he not know? Won't you confiscate the money?"

"Every dime. And we'll trace the money back to his sources in this country. You've given us a gold mine of information."

"The mother lode. But what happens when he learns it's gone. Or when the other five million is due? Will he come after me?"

"No."

"How can you be sure?

"We've had a bit of good luck. Did you meet the bookkeeper down there?"

"Oscar?"

"That's him. Oscar has been skimming. He was eager to defect. All we had to do was extricate him. We let him keep his own Cayman account and

221

the money he's skimmed, and set him up with a new identity in L.A."

Don smiled. "So when *Doble* discovers his money is gone, he'll think that Oscar took it."

"Exactly."

"I hope that new identity works. I wouldn't want to be Oscar if *Doble Venganza* ever gets hold of him. He's a cruel bastard."

Johns leaned forward and put his arms on the table. "My brother was an agent also."

"*Was* an agent?"

"He was undercover. When he was found out, *Doble Venganza* had him tortured. Tortured and murdered. In the most painful way you can imagine. As a warning to others."

"Like the men Trey saw executed in *Doble's* courtyard."

Johns nodded. "So I do know how cruel he can be."

Don was busy the next few weeks with the Trust's affairs. Prudo Kelley accepted Trey's resignation and appointed Eugene successor trustee of the family trust. It was a short session on the uncontested docket. Kelley had announced he was going to run for re-election after all and Richard Cator had settled for the safety of the District Attorney's office. He had even called to thank Don. It didn't hurt that Don had followed Jake's advice for once and sent campaign contributions to both their campaigns.

"I'm sorry for the misunderstanding, Cuinn," Cator said.

"That's ancient history, Richard," Don answered. "Let's get together for a beer sometime."

Judge Kelley looked stern when he signed the appointment. "Mr. Pervoy," he said to Eugene, "this is an important position of trust. Do you understand that?"

Don motioned for Eugene to stand up. "I guess I do, Your Honor," the rancher said, looking distinctly uncomfortable.

The judge continued, as if he were speaking to an unruly teenager. "You will be responsible for other people's money. You are in a position of trust toward them, a fiduciary. You are expected to adhere to the highest standard of care. Do you understand?"

"Yes, sir, I do," he said.

It's too bad nobody had that conversation with Trey, Don thought.

"Off the record now," the judge said to the court reporter. "Eugene, you and I have shared some very enjoyable evenings at the Country Club bar. My advice to you now is to stay home on Saturday nights."

Eugene turned and looked at Ginelle, then grinned sheepishly and said, "You ain't the first person to suggest that, Judge."

A week later they were back in Judge Kelley's courtroom for the hearing on whether the Pervoy trustee could sell the ranch's water rights.

Don and Eugene had exchanged seats with Jake. Wiley Franklin sat beside Jake, looking baffled by the turn of events.

Their case was called, and Don stood. "Good morning, Your Honor. I am Don R. Cuinn, representing Eugene L. Pervoy, Trustee of the Pervoy Family Trust, and also individually and as guardian of his minor children Kansas City..."

"Spare us the travelog, Mr. Cuinn. Your representation is noted." He turned to Jake. "I suppose you represent everybody else, Mr. Rosen."

"Yes, Your Honor, except for the unknown heirs and the unborn heirs of George Pervoy. Mr. Franklin has that honor."

"All right. Sit down, gentlemen. Let's see what we have here" He turned to Don. "Surprise me, Counselor, and tell me that your position hasn't changed. Or do you now think the trust permits the sale of the water rights?"

"That is the trustee's position, Your Honor. Also the other parties I represent."

"May I ask what led you to change your position, Mr. Cuinn?"

"Mr. Rosen's eloquent arguments, Your Honor, in addition to the fact that all the parties are ready to stipulate to that effect."

"What about the Rule Against Perpetuities? I thought I heard you argue earlier that the trust was void because it violated the Rule."

"I believe the trustee's duty is to argue for the trust's validity. Mr. Rosen apparently doesn't believe the Rule is an issue here." He turned to Jake, who nodded in agreement.

"That is correct, Judge," Jake said. "The most reasonable interpretation is that Mr. Pervoy intended the trust to last for the lives of his grandchildren plus twenty-one years."

The judge turned to Wiley, who was waiting like a man being led to the executioner's block. "That leaves you, Mr. Franklin. How do the unknowns and unborns feel about this? What's your position?"

Wiley cleared his throat. The computer printouts in his hand shook. "Ahem," he said, clearing his throat. He read from them. "The Rule Against Perpetuities is designed to prevent too remote vesting."

"What do you have there, Counselor?" Wiley handed him his notes. "Ah. *Corpus Juris Secundum.* The online version." He handed the notes back to Wiley. "The font of all knowledge."

Even with a Jeff Davis Law School degree, Don knew that CJS was a poor substitute for legal research. Not even a good starting place, and certainly not something you actually cited in a brief or in an argument.

"What have you concluded, Mr. Franklin, from your prodigious research?"

Wiley hesitated. Finally he said, "The authorities are split, Your Honor?"

The judge laughed and Don and Jake joined in. Wiley turned red, then laughed also. "They're split right down the middle, Your Honor. So I'd say that my clients the unborns think the trust is valid, and my clients the unknowns think it's void. And that's my position." With that he sat down.

Judge Kelley waited for the laughter to die down, then said, "I was really looking forward to a long, drawn-out battle of briefs about the Rule Against Perpetuities. I guess it's not to be." He picked up the draft order that Don had drafted. "It is hereby ordered and decreed that the Trustee of the George W. Pervoy Family Trust dated March 1, 1932, is empowered to sell, lease or otherwise dispose of all or any part of the water underlying the trust real estate known as the Pervoy Ranch."

"Any motions?" he said. He looked at Wiley who remained silent. "Good. Call the next case."

In the hall after the hearing, waiting for Ginelle to return from the ladies' room, Eugene said to Don and Jake, "I hate to sell that water. Daddy didn't want the ranch sold, and the water's part of the ranch. But there isn't no other way, is there?"

225

"No," Don answered. "There isn't. But maybe I can talk them into limiting the sale to fifty years. After that, the water rights would come back to the ranch. From what I understand, the buyers don't plan on producing the water, so your kids and grandkids might get the water back."

"Better than nothing," Eugene offered in way of thanks.

Jake spoke up. "You will never guess what Eugene and Ginelle have in mind for Trey's house."

"You're not moving up there?" Don had difficulty imagining them there.

"Oh, Hell, no," Eugene said. "This is Ginelle's idea. We're going to turn it into a retreat, you know for Dallas millionaires, to hunt and ride or just lay around and eat and drink. We're bringing in a big name chef from Houston to teach our Mexicans how to cook Mexican food."

"What does your mother think about it?"

"Oh, Mama don't know yet. But eventually she'll decide it was her idea. She can run the place. Not really run it, of course. Ginelle will do that. But Mama can be over there, entertaining the guests. Imagine, all those folks paying big money to hear Mama tell them about her family back in Longview."

After the hearing, Don stopped by Bridget's house. She poured them each a glass of wine, and they sat in the swing on the big front porch. Marcas was in Dallas on company business and Caitlin was inside watching television.

Bridget asked, "Are your dreams any better? Since your trip to Mexico?"

"I've looked the devil in the eye. I think we've done him some harm," he said. "It's not enough."

Bridget did not know the details of his trip to see the drug lord. She did know he had been able to free Trey from the cartel's clutches, but not to prevent his suicide.

The front porch light was on in the twilight. Bridget reached for his hand. "So, you are glad you went?"

"Yes." He squeezed her hand. "Bridget..."

She raised his hand to her lips and kissed it.

He went on. "I'm haunted. I probably always will be. But, that is, if you want to, I mean..."

"Do I want you to come in and have mad, mad sex with me?"

"You read my mind."

Lying in bed with Bridget, Don gave her a full account of his trip to Mexico, and of Bustin Johns' assurances that they were safe from cartel retaliation. "I wish I was as sure as he is. I hate to get you mixed up in all of this."

She smiled and said, "It's the government. What could possibly go wrong?"

He pulled her pale body against his and caressed her. "Would you like to go to Austin with me? I have some family business down there. We could visit the Thorpes. I could show you the town."

"Are you taking me home to meet your parents?"

He scooted down between her legs. "First, let's see if you really are a true redhead." He raised his head and said, "It's official, Red. I'm taking you home to meet my mama."

CHAPTER TWENTY-SIX

Don enjoyed watching Bridget with Dorrie Louise. They spoke the same female language immediately, most of it humorous remarks about Don, accompanied by giggling glances.

"Oh Donnie Ray," she laughed, "Dorrie Louise is going to show me your baby pictures."

"Show her the one of me on the pony, Mama. She doesn't believe I ever rode a horse."

It was Texas Relays weekend and the Haven Hotel was booked up. "What a rare thing," Dorrie Louise said. Instead she found them a room at the Old South Congress Avenue Motel, or the OSCA, pronounced like Katherine Hepburn saying "Oscar." It was owned and managed by Smythe Smithe, a poetess and one-time student of Papa's. She moved an unsuspecting assistant track coach out to make room for Professor Rothschild's son and his girl friend. She even gave them the T. S. Eliot suite, decorated with *Cats'* posters and passages from *The Waste Land*.

"I'm not sure if I can get an erection in the presence of such gayness," Don said to Bridget when they were alone.

"Sure you can," she answered.

The motel was in the center of the SOCA or South on Congress Avenue district. They strolled the crowded sidewalks, went into antique shops and jewelry stores and art galleries run by local artists. They stopped at a food trailer for a gelato. He guided her down the hill, past the School for the Deaf and Barton Springs Road to Auditorium Shores and the statue of Stevie Ray Vaughn. A kite-flying contest was in progress on the Great Lawn.

"I wonder where they got the name 'Great Lawn?' Oh, I see, this is Austin's answer to Central Park?"

"Snob," he answered. "You're from Velda, for God's sake."

"I read the *New York Times*," she answered.

They walked the trail along the shore of Lady Bird Lake, or as Don insisted on calling it, Town Lake, down to the Lamar bridge. The lake looked inviting. They climbed the pedestrian bridge and leaned against the metal railing, watching the action on the busy lake. They laughed at a couple trying to get their canoe out of the way of the Texas Longhorn women's rowing crew, out practicing in the sunshine. Up and down the riverside, the dogwood and redbud trees were in full blossom.

"Is it always like this in Austin?" Bridget asked, pulling down the brim of her baseball cap.

"Yes," he lied. "Every day."

She looked at him and shook her head. "You're a fraud."

"Probably. But this is the way I always think of it. Relays Weekend in Austin."

Later, over fried shrimp and oysters served on the deck of his favorite seafood restaurant, not far from the OSCA, she sipped her wine. She waited for the noise to die down, then leaned over close to him and asked, "Will you move back to Austin? You have to miss it."

"I don't think so. Strangely enough, I kind of like Velda."

"That doesn't seem strange to me."

"That's different. You were born there. You have Marcas and Caitlin, and yes, the major. You've made them your responsibility, one way or the other, and I love you for that. But I've made some interesting new friends there." He smiled and took her hand. "One in particular, who I don't think would be eager to move with me to Austin." He signaled the waiter for more wine. "Then there's Eugene. I don't want to abandon him."

"No. But still, your family is here."

"I'm a phone call away, if they need me. And of course, there's Jake. Now that I'm the lawyer for the Pervoy Trust, who used to be his biggest client, Jake has offered me a partnership."

"Really? You'd give up your empire in Antelope City?"

"We've talked about installing Wiley Franklin out there. I could look in on him every few days, and of course Maye would really be running the office. Another thing, the major called before we left. He asked if I could prepare some deeds of gift. He's making another round of endowments to the Velda Foundation." He looked at her. "But I bet you knew all about that. Is it your doing?"

"I wish I could take the credit. This is the first I've heard about it. You can be sure if Major Hansard wants you to do legal work for him, it's because he thinks you're a good lawyer."

"He may just think I have good taste in women." He watched the waiter re-fill their wine glasses. "I love it when you blush."

She took a sip. "Is it settled then? You're staying in Velda?"

"Seems like it. If you'll have me." He called for their check. "I need a nap. I want to show you Sixth Street tonight, and then tomorrow, we'll drive out and visit the Thorpes in Wimberley."

That night he took Bridget to his favorite bars on East Sixth. They drank Shiner Bock and listened

231

to music, Texas Rock, New Orleans Blues, Country Soul. They walked down the sidewalk and stood in front of Esther's Follies, watching the performers through the window. They looked admiringly at the athletes on the town after the Relays. They thought about taking a pedicab back to the hotel, but Bridget wanted to walk. Tipsy, they stumbled into bed at the OSCA and made sleepy love under a poster of Grizabella from the Broadway production of *Cats*.

It was mid-morning when Don woke. He turned on the machine and made himself a cup of coffee. He showered and dressed. Bridget slept through it all, snoring softly.

"Get dressed." He slapped her naked bottom. "We're due in Wimberley by afternoon."

"Quit that." She turned over in the bed and covered herself.

"You say this is called a 'duvet'?" he asked. He tugged it off and admired her. He thought about undressing but decided against it. "We need to go. I want to treat you to breakfast at Pedro's and then we're off to see the Thorpes."

At the famous Mexican restaurant on East Sixth, he pointed out prominent Texas politicians, introduced Bridget to Pedro's son and granddaughter, and insisted they have the *huevos rancheros*. It was early afternoon before they got through the Triangle onto Highway 290 so he could put the sporty orange Dodge Dart he had rented at the airport through its paces. "It's really an Alfa Romeo," he shouted over the road noise. He downshifted and the little Dodge jumped forward like a real sports car.

In Wimberley, he followed Elmer's directions through the little town and out the river road on the west bank of the Comal River. The river was flowing quietly, its deep blue waters reflecting the low-hanging branches of the huge Cypress trees.

"I can't believe this is here," she said. "It's a different world."

He followed the road according to Elmer's directions and slowed down when he came to the Antelope City city limits sign. The population number had been painted over in red with the number "2". "I wondered where that sign went," Don said.

"I'll bet you sent it to him," she said.

He pulled the Dart into a large circular drive surrounded by a lawn of St. Augustine grass. He parked in front of the three-car garage. The garage doors were open. In one space, they could see the license plates on a red Cadillac. The plate read "Hers." Next to it was a Ford F-150 pick-up truck. Its license plate read "Who Cares?"

Elmer came out from behind the truck, carrying a bag of charcoal briquettes. Don was startled to see the old rancher's knobby knees and skinny calves protruding from a pair of burnt orange shorts. The shorts were set off by a matching University of Texas polo shirt. Elmer put down the bag with a grin, wiped his hands on his shorts and wobbled over. He hugged Bridget and whispered something in her ear. She giggled.

"Watch it, old man," Don said.

A little awkwardly, Elmer hugged him. "I knew her before you did," he said. "Much too good for you." He pointed to the house. "Come in, Come in. Lou Jo's about busted a gut, she's so excited to see you."

Lou Jo met them at the door, resplendent in a gold lame pants suit. Her expensively coiffured hair was bleached bright blonde and her wrinkles had disappeared. "She must have had the best plastic surgeon in Las Vegas," Bridget said to Don when they were alone. "The best that oil money can buy," he answered.

Even her voice had toned down, the voice of money overlaying her Panhandle twang. "Get in this house, you two," she said, holding the door open. Two toy poodles yapped at her feet. Don looked at Elmer, who shrugged.

The house was a massive sprawl of cream-colored Austin limestone and redwood. Giant stone fireplaces graced the living room, the den, the formal dining room, the breakfast room and the screened back porch. White leather furniture was everywhere. An expensive interior designer had been at work. Lou Jo installed them in the guest suite, complete with its own sitting room, fireplace, large screen TV, and hotel style kitchen. "Put on your bathing suits and come down to the river. Elmer's making martinis and we're going tubing."

Don and Bridget floated in the cool Blanco River, sipping their martinis from giant acrylic glasses. The dogs chased tree branches that Elmer threw for them. Lou Jo put her brightly painted toenails in the water, shivered and retreated to her lounge chair. Elmer brought out brick-size sirloin steaks and seasoned them for grilling.

"I thought you were moving to Dripping Springs," Don said to the old rancher.

"She didn't like the name."

Lou Jo chimed in. "Damn if I'm going to tell people that we live in some place called Drip when I write my annual Christmas letter. There's only one Drip around here," she said, pointing at Elmer, "and that's him."

234

After dinner, they sat in front of a roaring fire. "Turn that air conditioner down lower," Lou Jo ordered. Elmer got up and fiddled with the controls.

Lou Jo took a polite Bridget to the bedroom to see some new satin sheets. "They're French," she said by way of explanation.

Don accepted another brandy. "So this is home, after all those moves," he said. "No more re-divorces?"

"That's all in the past," the old man said, rubbing his kneecap. "I love that woman."

CHAPTER TWENTY-SEVEN

Don sat in the little library near the front entrance of the Haven Hotel. He put down the news section of the morning paper. The lead story reported that Sawbucks Banjo had completed the sale of his water rights to a combine of Texas cities. *The Antelope Play didn't kill his deal after all*, Don thought.

He re-read the sales contract, which he had examined earlier in the day, just to be sure. Dorrie Louise had been offered good money to sell the struggling hotel. The buyer wanted to tear it down and build an upscale apartment house. When Lena, Don's stepmother and Dorrie Louise's protector, died, she left the hotel to Dorrie Louise. Dorrie Louise had promised to keep a place there for Lena's poet husband, retired university professor Ralph Rothschild. But Papa was in a wheelchair now and wanted to move to a retirement home on the other side of the University. They would take the money from the sale of the Haven and buy a two-bedroom apartment in the Cartwright House, where Dorrie Louise would continue to care for the aging professor.

"All his old buddies are there," Dorrie Louise said. His mother's hair was completely gray now, but she was as thin and spry as ever. "But am I going against Lena's wishes? Am I doing a bad thing?"

Don had examined the hotel books. It was obviously a failing business. The offer was good, better than Don would have hoped. "Lena was a pragmatist. This poor place is done. Sell it and quit killing yourself trying to keep it open."

"What about you, Donnie Ray? Are you going to stay in the cold country?"

"It's not the Arctic, Mama. To tell you the truth, I'm beginning to like it up there. On most days, there's a gentle breeze all day, and when you stand in an old elm tree's shade, it's cool. You can see forever, beautiful, beautiful wildflowers and prairie grasses. Eroded streams run bank to bank after a rain." He folded the sales contract and put it back in its folder. He was satisfied with it.

"The country's not monotonous at all, not really. Every time you look at it, it's changed. The colors, the shadows, the rocks. Usually, it's a very calm place. Then along comes a big storm, a lightning storm with tornados on the horizon, or a big blizzard with snow drifts as high as this house and there's all this excitement. But as soon as it's over, it's calm again." He handed her the folder. "If I were you, I'd sell."

"So it's the scenery?"

"Well, I also like the people."

"Especially one person in particular, right?"

"I won't deny it. I think she can fill a big hole in my heart."

"It's time, Donnie Ray. Let it happen. If it makes any difference, Papa and I both like her very much."

She bustled back to the kitchen. Don found a slender volume of Papa's poems and sat down to read. He was almost through the first poem when he looked up and saw Bustin Johns.

"Got a minute?" the federal agent asked.

"Of course," Don said, closing the book. "What are you doing here?"

"I have something to show you." He pulled up a chair and opened his tablet. He turned it so

238

Don could read the screen. On it was a report, labeled "Top Secret." It read:

Venganza Cartel Leaders Victim of Attack by Rival Gang? Mexican authorities report that Acapulco area hospitals have been treating an unusual series of suspicious illnesses. Just as unusual, the patients are all well-known members of the powerful Venganza drug cartel. Their symptoms have included nausea, hair loss, throat swelling and pallor. Over the course of a few weeks, the patients have experienced multiple organ failure, including the liver, kidneys and bone marrow. None are expected to survive.

The victims include Jose Luis Gomez, known as Doble Venganza, his half-brother, Pedro, known as Ojos Tortuga, and twenty-five high-ranking members of the cartel leadership. "Venganza is no more; it's gone" one police authority said.

U.S. sources report that Mexican authorities believe the symptoms are typical of radiation poisoning and that the Venganza leaders are dying a hideous death. If it was radiation poisoning, it represents the first use of radioactive material in the violent wars between the cartels fighting to the death for control of the drug trade to the United States.

"Wow!" Don said. "Radiation poisoning? Really?"

"Are you familiar with the death of the Russian KBG agent, Alexander Litveninko?"

"No."

"The Brits believe he was poisoned by Polonium-210 placed in his tea. And Yasser Arafat is rumored to have been poisoned with it."

239

"Polonium what?"

"Polonium-210. It's a very rare element. It is made in nuclear reactors. Extremely small doses are lethal if it is ingested. Less than 1 gram is sufficient to kill. Once it's in the bloodstream, it's nearly impossible to stop. The surest way to poison someone with Polonium-210 is for the victim to consume it in food or drink, like the Russian's tea, which he drank at a London hotel."

"Would Scotch work?" Don asked.

"Oh, yes," the agent replied.

"How long does it take?" Don was counting the number of days since he left the *Venganza* headquarters.

"With a minimum lethal dose, that's 0.89 micrograms, just an almost invisible speck, no visible effect would be seen for about a week, with mild symptoms developing over the next week. Serious illness would not be expected for a month or more. Death would be expected from the poisoning within two or three months."

Don closed the tablet and handed it back to Johns. "Okay. How did you do it? You did do it, didn't you?"

"The United States government does not poison its enemies. We might kill them with a drone, but we do not poison them."

"I didn't say the government did it. I said you did it. You sent me down there with poisoned Scotch to get revenge for your brother's death. God. I might have drunk some myself. That's why you told me to stick to tequila! How did you get hold of the stuff?"

"A small quantity of Polonium-210 has gone missing from the Oak Ridge Lab. We have given the Mexicans information that it was stolen by an agent of an important Mexican general."

"Let me guess. The general is rumored to have ties to a rival drug ring."

"Oh, it's not a rumor."

"Your cover story is that this general had the *Venganzas* poisoned?"

"Well, he does have an agent here. The agent has confirmed the story on a video tape we gave the Mexicans."

"This 'agent'—is he an actor or some poor illegal who doesn't want to be sent home?"

Johns smiled tightly. "As I said, this agent has confirmed that he gave Polonium-210 to some unknown person working for the general. How the poison got into the Scotch whiskey, we don't know."

"You do know how it got in there. Tell me."

"It does not help the general's cause that a large transfer of funds has been made to his private account."

"From the cartel's Cayman Island accounts?"

"Who can say? So many accounts. So many layers."

"But how did you get it in the Scotch? It's radioactive. Have I been poisoned too? Have you?"

"It's interesting. Polonium-210 can be handled safely. It's only dangerous if it is ingested. For example, someone could use a very thin titanium hypodermic needle to insert a lethal dose into a sealed bottle of Scotch, with absolutely no risk of radiation poisoning. The hole would not be visible, especially if a new tax stamp was placed on it. A person could handle that bottle, even open it, with no danger at all. No one would ever know."

"I know."

"All you know, and what I came to Austin to tell you, is that *Doble Venganza* is dead. He suffered

241

a terrible punishment for the murders he committed.

"Your brother."

"And your wife."

THE END

ABOUT THE AUTHOR

BOYD TAYLOR lives in Austin, Texas with his wife. This is the second novel in his Donnie Ray Cuinn series. In a former life, he was a lawyer and an officer of a large chemical company. He worked for a number of years in the Texas Panhandle. A native of Temple, Texas, he graduated from the University of Texas at Austin with a BA in government and an LLB from the law school. A third Donnie Ray Cuinn novel is in the works.

Boyd welcomes inquiries and comments from his readers, who may contact him through Katherine Brown Press at kbtpress@ymail.com or on his Facebook page at:

www.facebook.com/TheHeroofSanJacinto

CPSIA information can be obtained at www.ICGtesting.com
Printed in the USA
LVOW12s0219130713

342624LV00005B/8/P